HAVEN

HAVEN

GRAEME BENNETT

Published by Graeme Bennett Ltd.

CONTENTS

CONTENTS

Preface

The story told in book one ("Helix") focused on the plight of refugees and the technologically disenfranchised. Book two brings a new perspective: that of the leaders and the wealthy. It's a view of how the customs and cultures of the world are rapidly changing due to the social and economic shifts we see today. It's the other side of the story of the gap between the 'haves' and the 'have nots.'

Whereas, in the first book, those adhering to a religious orthodoxy struggled to maintain their beliefs in the face of technological change as new disruptors such as artificial biodiversity and artificial intelligence further estranged them from the status quo, here we see the machinations of those actually pulling the strings and redefining the rules. This is a 'social science fiction' story of how the wealthiest and most influential members of society are increasingly driving the cultural and societal shifts that lead to a world in which the political systems and market dynamics are largely controlled by an elite group of multinational corporations. Herein lie the artifacts and ruins of this possible future.

Enjoy the dig.

Graeme Bennett

November 16, 2023

Moving Forward

> *Who dreamt and made incarnate*
> *gaps in Time & Space?*
>
> —ALAN GINSBERG

Andrew remembered the first time he met his grandmother. She'd offered him a place to stay if he ever wanted to come to the Bay Area for a visit. And so, not long after he'd learned to drive, he made his first epic journey—a 16-hour marathon road trip from Vancouver to visit her in Berkeley. When he arrived, the first thing she did was give him a big hug and apologize for the mess. Her apartment smelled like the patchouli-scented birthday cards he'd received as a child. It was all a bit rococo, with paisley-patterned sheets hanging like canopies above the bed and on the walls. A thick Indian-motif carpet. And huge pillows everywhere.

"Grandma Stern…" he began.

"Oh please," she laughed, her rosy cheeks bunching up a little near her eyes, "call me Lilly. 'Grandma Stern' is, oh I don't know, somebody who sounds much older than me. I'm just Lilly, with two 'l's. Short for Lillian."

"Do you mind telling me a little about Grampa?" he asked.

She told him how she and Thomas Stern had met at school in Berkeley during the 1960s peace-and-love era. Two summers later, they were living together. Petting a cat, she remembered how she had just sat down at the kitchen table in their third-floor apartment (above a newly opened head shop named Annapurna) not far from the Berkeley campus when Thomas announced the big news about his new government-funded position.

Lilly brought Andrew a plate of small green logs she called 'grape leaves wrap in olive oil' and a bowl of what looked like yogurt. She continued with her story as he spooned his way through the warm yogurt soup, trying not to make faces.

"Your father had just been born," she told Andrew, "and suddenly my husband wasn't allowed to speak about exactly what he did at work anymore. And then in the heat of an argument, I used what I thought was a ridiculous example: that I was stuck here breastfeeding while he was off 'building H-bombs.' And then," she remembered bitterly, "came the reply that blew up everything: 'And what if I was?'"

"Sure, I was a bit more of a hippie than he was," she admitted, "and sure, we'd met while we were both in the nuclear science graduate program, but how," she wondered aloud, "could a person go from working in a restaurant where patrons thought it was meaningful that the name looked like

'GOD POT' from inside the window to bomb builder for the military-industrial complex?"

And, Andrew silently mused, how could his own father go down the same path 40 years later and not expect a similar result?

"Your grandfather was very charming and handsome when I met him at the university's student union building, you know. He introduced himself as Tom, but said his friends all called him Thomas," she laughed, her eyes sparkling. He was, she said admiringly, a brilliant theoretical scientist working on his PhD at the Lawrence Berkeley National Laboratory. "They call it Berkeley Lab now," she explained, "but back then, we just called it the Lawrence Lab. His field of specialty was quantum field theory. You know, one of his associates—we'd had her over for dinner a few times—called me up one day, quite concerned. She said she wasn't the only one who'd noticed that he'd seemed kind of depressed or, you know, something just wasn't quite right, and she was just calling to see if everything was all right. As it turned out, he *wasn't* okay. Most nights, he was up half the night pacing the floor, he couldn't sleep, he barely stopped working to eat. I really got to hate the sound of that typewriter. He'd been studying like crazy with this incredible workload and I was pregnant and... well, it was a really hard time for him."

"He'd call me from work late at night and I'd just say, 'come home, come to bed,' y' know? He was working on a bunch of advanced calculations for his thesis and had devised some tests designed to provide proof for a radical variant of string theory that he hoped would get him a good position somewhere, you know? And the poor man was just falling apart the whole time."

"And then when the baby came, he wasn't getting enough sleep and I wasn't working and the money got tight and, well, it just got worse and worse."

"At that point, it seemed clear that he wasn't ready to be a responsible father. I was pretty demanding in those days, and I guess I shouldn't have forced him to have to choose between his family or the work he loved. But, you know, I just couldn't accept the idea of him working for the military, building H-bombs or whatever. It was a scary time and I wanted no goddamned part of it—and it was certainly not the world I wanted for my child. So, I left him and drove all the way to Canada just to keep Isaac away from the bombs and the draft and the war and everything."

"In retrospect, staying in Canada without a work visa or social security was probably a pretty bad idea, but nobody really seemed to care much about that back then. I got a job at a vegetarian café and shared a big ol' house with a few people, and it was a good area for Isaac to grow up in, for a few years at least."

She fiddled absent-mindedly with the silver and jade ring on her little finger as if tuning in some old memories. "After the draft ended in January of '73, I was a little less paranoid about bringing him back to the U.S. and so I sort of tentatively came back to Berkeley to sign the divorce papers and, well, I guess my heart had always been here, y'know? I figured it was better for Isaac to be in his own country. And Thomas was making a stink about me keeping Isaac away from him.

He didn't like that. I was not very kind to him around then, I must admit."

She shrugged. "So maybe goin' to Canada was not the best move for me, but I sure think it was the right move for *your* mother, and I'll defend that to my grave. Your mother did the right thing, one hundred percent."

Grandma Stern had broken up with her Thomas over the very same concerns Andrew's own mother had when she left Isaac and moved to Canada. It wasn't the life Lilly thought she'd seen in her husband's idealistic young eyes, back when they were both students at UC Berkeley's science program, and it wasn't the life Andrew's mother wanted, either. She never turned her back on her ideology, and Andrew respected that.

In fact, it had been Lilly Stern who had urged her daughter-in-law to help Andrew avoid conscription (or, she worried, some future draft) by moving to Canada.

A few hours later, Andrew said goodbye (for the last time, as it turned out) and stood on the corner of Telegraph Avenue near the Caffe Mediterraneum, where his father told him how he, as a young man, had listened to Allan Ginsberg earnestly shouting peyote-inspired poetic nonsense about incarnate gaps in time and space.

Andrew remembered his father clipping a radiation dosimeter badge to his shirt when he took him to visit the controlled areas of the facility as a small child. And when he excitedly told his mother about it, she chastised him and gave him a lecture on how government-funded nuclear research had torn their family apart. Twice. He'd gotten mad at her that day and vowed that when he was in charge, things would be different. She was being foolish anyway. The good that had come from such research far outweighed the downsides. Had it been living in Canada all those years that had turned her into such a peacenik?

o o o

Thomas Stern had encouraged his son to study the sciences and Isaac had finished a master's degree program at UC Berkeley. He studied physics at the insistence of his father, and the fantastically high tuition costs paid off when he secured a position in a minor role on the Bevatron team at Berkeley Lab. It wasn't much, but it was a start.

While working at the lab, Isaac worked toward a business administration degree and, four years later, held an MBA degree and gave up his father's dream of a professorship or doctorate title. He had taken an avid interest in the business of high-stakes research facility funding, though. He continued to work, in increasingly significant roles, on the original Bevatron until its last years. When it finally closed, he was offered a position at the Research Campus of Princeton University to help launch their synchrotron project.

His father insisted that the opportunity to stand close to where towering intellects such as Einstein and Gödel had stood was too compelling to pass up—but Isaac saw its proximity to New York and Washington DC as the key attraction. In those days, government and private sector financing for quantum research was plentiful—especially on the east coast.

With no other accelerator options in the western U.S., it was the obvious choice.

It was only after Isaac accepted the position that he learned that his father was the lease-holder on the 300-acre property upon which the facility was built. He also owned a pair of houses on adjacent lots—properties acquired when land north of Trenton was cheap in the early 1970s.

The idea of moving away from beautiful Berkeley nagged him but two months later he handed in his apartment key and moved to Princeton, New Jersey.

As it was four months until the lab was scheduled to open,

and they wouldn't even be ready for him to start work for almost two months, Isaac spent some time in the late spring exploring the area.

He headed for the coast and found Toms River and, beyond it, the boardwalk and beaches in Seaside Heights. There wasn't much activity taking place in the restaurants and bars along the boardwalk at that time of the year. Of course, there were always a few kids—dropouts, mostly—drawn there by the fast food and readily available part-time jobs. Some were looking for work and some were just bored. The local kids knew there was easy money available for anyone willing to scrub awnings or repaint a weather-beaten wall. The old guys would show them how to operate the cotton candy machines and the deep fryers. The more ambitious ones were trained as "arcade attendants" and taught how to lure the suckers into the casinos or the "dollar a throw" arcades and "win a prize every time" amusements. Here they were, on that first weekend in June, the hawkers and carnies hanging up their stuffed animals on the midway, and the kids, busily prepping the weather-worn walls for a fresh coat of paint.

Everything was about to change. In a few weeks, the pier would be bustling with activity, the air filled with the smells of corn dogs and beer. The beachside bars would be filled with hard-partying New Yorkers and the midway packed with kids celebrating the end of the school year or anything else.

On that first weekend after the schools got out, it seemed like everyone under the age of 30 showed up. They came *en masse* to a full-time party on the pier that kept going all summer long. On the July fourth weekend, the traffic and the crowds were utterly insane. The cops would confiscate fireworks from the kids and then set them off themselves. The parking enforcement officers were ever-present, taking full advantage of the 15-minute parking spot limitations and handing out tickets for even the most trivial or momentary infractions. Even those *obeying* the 9 p.m. beach curfew would be ticketed if they were still on the beach when the bell sounded. It was a great time to invite a lady or two to join you elsewhere—there was live music in the bars and weekend partiers with painted lips and smoky eyes, eager to be spoiled.

Isaac thought back to the time he'd slept over at a new lady-friend's beach house. "I paid $1500 last month to rent this place," she told him. "Next week, the price goes up to $2500 a *week*."

It's worth it, he thought, marveling at the waterfront view from the porch. "That's quite a jump. Where are you going to go?"

Her name was Maria and her parents had recently separated. Her father was apparently a well-to-do investment banker; her mother had grown up near the old Diamond Alkali chemical plant site in Newark, near the banks of the notoriously polluted Passaic River. Maria had introduced Isaac to her mother but quietly explained to him that her mom had recently been diagnosed with a brain tumor and wasn't expected to live long. She blamed it on the toxic waste: specifically, the high levels of dioxins in the area's groundwater. Every other week, workers at the plant had dumped dioxins and other chemical waste byproducts into trenches that flowed into the Passaic; in all, the old factory was dumping 20,000 tons of toxic chemicals into the ground every year. And the chemical waste had leeched into soil and the water supply. Lawsuits were as prevalent as the cancers, she said. So they moved. And then, when mom got sick, dad moved out.

"Oh, I'm going to stay with my sister in Toms River," she said. "But I'll rent this place again next spring if it's available again. I *love* having a beach house. And a boat."

"You have a boat?"

She looked at him as if to say *of course*. "It's actually my dad's, but he lets me use it."

"Well, let's go!"

○ ○ ○

Ironically, it was that boat that both marked the beginning and the end of what had been Isaac's first serious relationship. They'd had fun that summer, taking the sailboat out quite regularly for afternoon jaunts around the bay until one afternoon, when all it took was a poorly executed jibe to discover that the cables holding the mast up were connected to blocks screwed into weather-rotted wood. The mast moorings—first one, then the others—broke loose and down it came into the water. And the weight of the sinking mast pulled the boat over and the hapless sailors along with it into the drink. After her father found out that the new boyfriend had sunk his boat, the relationship met a similar fate.

After they broke up, Isaac returned to Princeton and doubled down on his business administration efforts and before long had built a credible reputation as a leadership candidate for the MPACTD group at Princeton. Senior researcher Dr.

Jonathon Majors was currently in that position. He was a decent researcher, sure, but he didn't take direction well. And he had absolutely no vision. Several members of the team under the direction of Dr. Majors, Isaac learned, had struggled under his 'style' of leadership. Majors had been critical of Stern's call for a new approach to the problem, and had convened a meeting with the board of directors of the science committee to discuss the issue. It was at that meeting where Isaac got his big break.

Jonathon's wife answered the phone that morning. "It's the university," she shouted up the stairs.

"Just a minute." He picked up the extension phone. "Hello."

"Dr. Jonathon Majors?"

"Yes?"

"We need you at a meeting today at 11 a.m. Can you attend? It's urgent."

"Yes. What is the meeting about?"

"It's a tribunal meeting. We'll explain more at 11 a.m., in the Dean's office. See you then."

"I'll be there."

His wife was standing in the doorway as he hung up the phone. "Hmm," he said. "*Something's* up."

When Majors arrived, the department head, the Dean's administrative assistant and three members of his team were in the waiting room outside the Dean's office. At 11 a.m., the assistant opened the door and they all went in. Inside, the Dean sat behind his desk with his hands folded.

"Thank you all for attending on such short notice. I'll get

straight to the point. We've had several reports in recent weeks of, uh, concerns over the direction of the department. As that falls to you, Dr. Majors, we'd like you to, uh, take some time off to rethink the strategic direction. You're eligible for a paid sabbatical, so let's say twelve months. During that period, I'm appointing Isaac Stern as interim director. And we'll do a formal evaluation in twelve months' time."

"Pardon me, sir, but I must object," insisted Dr. Majors. "We are too close to cracking those field equations," he asserted. "Twelve months is practically an eternity in this field. Fidor at CERN almost has this problem cracked; we'll forfeit our advantage if I step down now. I won't go."

"I'm sorry Jonathon. If you don't take the sabbatical, I'm taking you off the project for twelve months of *unpaid* leave. Isaac, what is your response to Dr. Majors' concerns?"

"I have an agreement-in-principle with Dr. Erich Rössler, to bring him in to lead this project, and I will manage the overall budget and scale our efforts appropriately in support of his efforts. That, I believe, will prove to be a winning combination for the university and its industry partners alike."

"Jonathon and Isaac, if the two of you would be kind enough to step into the waiting room for a moment, we'll vote on this. My administrator will accompany you. Thank you."

The administrator followed them out and shut the door quietly behind her.

"A show of hands please," said the Dean, "All those in favor of Isaac Stern taking over as interim director for a period of twelve months while Dr. Majors is on sabbatical?"

The dept. head, one of Majors' team members and the

Dean raised their hands. The two other members of the team sided with Majors.

"The motion is carried. All right, let's get them back in here."

"Please enjoy your sabbatical, Doctor. I look forward to seeing you in twelve months' time."

Jonathon saw the expressions on the faces of his two supporters and shook his head. "Thank you, Dean," he said quietly as he turned to leave.

The vote of non-confidence saw Majors ousted from the position of team leader and Isaac Stern and his golden boy, Dr. Erich Rössler, were in.

Fresh from his successes on the team that discovered nuclear antimatter and the first known example of a lack of symmetry in nature, Isaac now had both the credentials and the connections to attract investor interest, not to mention the interest of a woman who would become the mother of his children.

In those days, Isaac spent a lot of time commuting between Princeton and Brookhaven, but in the summer of 1999, he took a working vacation to Vancouver, Canada, to visit the site of what was at that time the world's largest cyclotron, dubbed TRIUMF.

"I don't really know what a cyclotron is,
but I am certainly very happy Canada has one"

— *Pierre Trudeau, the 15th Prime Minister of Canada,
at the TRIUMF commissioning ceremony*

It was there that Isaac met Caroline Murray, a young researcher at the facility and a recent graduate from the nearby University of British Columbia. She knew of the Bevatron and was full of questions. A lunch invitation led to subsequent dinner dates and, a few weeks later, she accepted his invitation to visit his new facility in Princeton. A year later, they were married and she took the name Mrs. Caroline Stern.

o o o

2

Breakthrough

The universal principle which as the balance between finiteness and infinity, stability and flexibility underlies self-similar fractal forms emerging at the 'edge of chaos' indeed seems to be the Golden Ratio Spiral.

— MARJA DE VRIES

The company formerly known as the quantum physics research lab at Princeton University had launched with a modestly successful IPO, based on a portfolio of intellectual properties gained in large part from the advanced quantum field theory research done by its top graduate students over the past eight years.

It had gained some attention in the popular press due to its unwillingness to confirm or deny reports that it had successfully neutralized a source of Cherenkov radiation. (Several supposedly "science-focused" publications and most of the popular media left the name 'Cherenkov' out of the sensational headlines, of course.) Despite a roster of admirable projects, the board of directors had decided that its previous emphasis on pure research was not sustainable. But there was money in "practical" applications and military and space-based scenarios such as ion thruster research, A.I.–based expert systems, quantum communications, high-energy magnetic field effects and energy weapons. And so, Isaac Stern, CEO of the fledgling company, was tasked with transforming it from an academic research facility into a money-making investor magnet.

One of the things that had to change was the company's original name. The group's first big research effort had been a study of "M-Theoretical Particle Asymmetry Corresponding to T-Duality" and, for a while, the research group was known as MPACTD for a while as a nod to that. However, as a company name, that just wasn't going to cut it. Stern pitched the name "MPAX" as a replacement. Like its predecessor, he argued, the new name suggested important, high-impact research, and strongly evoked the concept of collider research: particle acceleration and nuclear particle impact detection. "It is a name that reflects the future of the company," he argued. The board of directors agreed, and so MPAX it was.

That was, until much of the research shifted away from particle physics to quantum field theory. Suddenly, the idea that particles are epiphenomena arising from fields and, indeed, the notion that there are no particles, there are only fields, became something more than a fringe theory. Suddenly, it wasn't about high-speed particle acceleration any more.

Again, the name wasn't a comfortable fit. It was decided that HELX—ostensibly an acronym for 'high energy large accelerator'—was a better name. However, the quantum field generator project that had originally been thought of as a secondary function for the accelerator had, by this time, become one of its most important and promising features. Some of the directors on the board argued that "QFG" would make a better name. Others thought it sounded like a brand of fried chicken or a grocery chain. The QFG wasn't the company's only important asset, though.

Biotech was hot—especially Messenger RNA tech. That became the house specialty of a new biotech division that roused the stock price as it joined two other new divisions, focusing on 'business AI' and quantum field research, respectively. Stern managed to snag Erich Rössler, lured by generous stock options, to lead the HELX group on an energetic light project. That soon morphed into a broader role, overseeing the entire quantum research division.

Rössler ended up managing both the DevOps teams, led by an ambitious young Austrian named Karl Schraeder, and the engineering teams. One of his first actions was to promote recent MIT Honors grad Li Yan Zhang to head of engineering. He also hired a young intern named Amir Roy as a meeting coordinator, project planning assistant and all-around gopher.

o o o

Did you know?

George Gunderson, the graduate student who had come

up with the method of neutralizing Cherenkov radiation, unwittingly signed over the rights to the invention when he signed up for a job at the research lab spinoff organization that became HELX. That tech proved invaluable in solving the key problem of achieving the necessary frequencies that allowed the high energy light accelerator to outperform much larger linear accelerators and other competing technologies.

○ ○ ○

Although the hiring had happened quickly, these were by no means hasty decisions. Rössler had been keeping an eye on these up-and-comers for several months and felt certain that they were the right people for the positions he needed to fill. These decisions, in large part, proved remarkably prescient. They did indeed work well together, and learned the AI control routines quickly.

And then something remarkable happened. While testing a new AI-generated field generation routine based upon a multidimensional vector math algorithm developed by a young mathematics genius named Susan Everett, a temporal disturbance was experienced and the clock instantly jumped ahead 17 seconds.

○ ○ ○

The big breakthrough was something of a technological confluence that solved a problem that had plagued time-travel theorists for more than a century: how to achieve the necessary speed (in this case, the wavelength frequency) without nearly infinite power consumption—and without having to travel somewhere at the speed of light to achieve it. The AI's solution substituted frequency for distance in the speed-of-light equation. Everett's algorithm posited that time itself was, as Einstein had once written, "dimensional *like space*"—in other words, multidimensional. And once the wavefield was suitably energized to the target frequency, it behaved exactly as particles would if traveling at that speed in space-time. Once again, the purity of the math behind this hidden truth was revealed as a simple equivalency—a manifestation of wave/particle duality in action.

Over the next few years, Gunderson and the others on Rössler's team developed solutions that allowed the safe transfer of organic matter and data forward through time-accelerating quantum fields. Initially, these quantum field generation efforts required a warehouse-sized field generator and used massive amounts of power; later refinements resulted in a more energy-efficient mobile platform that could be used virtually anywhere.

Isaac Stern's star, too, was ascending. The company's portfolio of public projects such as superconducting accelerators and free-electron lasers was interesting and fresh enough to attract investor interest, but what really caught the attention of the speculators was the undisclosed but widely rumored work that was going on for its government and military partners.

Hush-hush military contracts like this were, of course, a boon for the company. Isaac upgraded to a Bentley Mulsanne and dreamt of one day owning a Rolls-Royce Phantom VIII. The chairs in his office were updated from the ones that had been advertised as being made with "the finest Corinthian leather." What a disappointment it had been to learn that there was no such thing. The term, as it turned out, was nothing more than a marketing executive's fantasy. And so out they went.

In addition to the office environment and the branding of the company, Isaac also upgraded his aspirations and expectations. A new executive assistant/office manager/godsend named Rona filed and typed, sure, but she managed details like no one else. And that enabled Isaac to better organize the company at scale. He assembled a competent and well-connected board of directors, including leaders from the academic and business worlds and spent a year pitching to venture capitalists on both coasts. It wasn't long before he had the funds to go after the bigger fish. He built the right connections with the consortiums and they hooked up someone from DARPA and the next thing you know, the U.S. government was knocking.

3

The Machinery of Night

> *Physicists ought to put a special sign in their offices to remind themselves of how much they don't know. The message on the sign would be very simple. It would consist entirely of one word, or, rather, number: 137.*
>
> —RICHARD FEYNMAN

Rona rushed to Isaac's office and spoke in a hushed voice. Two men in military garb—a Lieutenant Colonel R. 'Bob' Baker and a Major Alan Jamison, said their business cards— had arrived, reported Rona in a hushed voice. They'd introduced themselves by saying they represented the "consortium of consortiums" known as Cornerstone.

"Send them in, thank you."

Isaac pulled the clutter into his top drawer and stood up just as the door opened. "Please come in." He shook their hands and gestured past the chairs to a pair of upholstered leather couches and a coffee table in a V shape in the far corner. "Sit wherever you like. May I offer you some water or coffee? Or something else to drink, perhaps?"

"Coffee sounds good right about now," said Baker.

"Me too, thanks," said Jamison.

Cornerstone's mandate, they explained, covered numerous sectors, including advanced technology, aircraft, radar and electronic warfare, ground vehicles, soldier systems, cyber tech, optics, radiological and nuclear.

Like any successful executive, Stern had learned the easy rhythm of the assured businessperson, subtly showing off the gears of a well-oiled machine. Rona smiled as she brought in a tray with three coffees, cream, sugar and stir sticks, then left again silently.

The lieutenant colonel got straight to the point. "We received your proposal and wanted to come down and talk about it a little. Thank you for meeting with us today, sir."

"My pleasure."

"We were grateful for your father's involvement across several government contracts, back in the day," he said. "Lucky to have him on our side."

Stern smiled as Baker explained that this sort of science was more of the Major's area of expertise. Alan Jamison leaned forward. "We've heard you are doing some great work on energetic light and quantum fields. Those are areas we're very interested in. In fact, we have a very specific interest in advanced math for our quantum field projects. We're looking for the very best."

"These people here are all under contract to HELX, y'understand?"

"Of course. We take good care of our partners, Mr. Stern."

"Gentlemen, the fact that you're here today tells me that we can help you achieve success in your temporal research projects. I know you've been working on this sort of thing for a long time and I want to assure you that we have the missing piece of that puzzle. And that piece will put the US in a world leadership position in what I think you'll agree is the most strategically significant development in human history. Hell, this thing's bigger than the A-bomb. Way bigger than that in its implications."

So, you think two years is a reasonable estimate?"

"Yes, we've already got a solid proof of concept working here. And, in addition to that two-year patent license, that 14.6 billion dollars gets you the source code to what we have working today, of course. And then, if you choose to have us deliver a working implementation of the current prototype, then that is an additional 18.2 billion dollars. And that gets you five additional years on the patent and all required staffing–not including the location or facility cost."

His speech patterns were full of enthusiastic-sounding buzzwords. He talked of 'incentivizing disruptive innovation' and 'drilling down to enhance the discoverability of key customer personas by focusing on actionable analytics.' He teased his newest innovation as 'the mother of all game-changers.' And while this type of vacuous execu-speak made him the subject of private ridicule among many of his subordinates, for a certain class of corporate customer, it worked.

Stern's proposal made it clear that, even with those costs added, his offering compared very favorably with the estimated 52.86-billion-dollar cost of the LHC project at CERN.

"Yes, that's all very clear in here, thank you for the detailed summary—it helps us make our case with our superiors. So, we'll seek approval for this on our end. I think we can go ahead and schedule a follow-up on this. Can we meet your team leader later this week?"

"Yes, we'll line up everyone on our end here right away and confirm it with your office by end of day. I'll get on the horn with my department head, right away, and we'll meet here again with you on... Shall we say Thursday? Is that too soon?"

"No, that sounds fine. The sooner the better."

"How 'bout Thursday morning, 11 a.m.?" Stern knew that Erich was preoccupied with hiring staff, but he was sure he could get him to attend.

"That'll work."

"Would you like a little tour of the place?"

"By all means. On Thursday after the meeting. How'd that be? I'm sure we'll have a few questions."

"Great. Do you think an hour will be enough?"

"Could we say an hour and a half, just to be on the safe side? You'll have your people there, yes?

"Absolutely. You know Dr. Erich Rössler. I'll make sure he's there in person. Will you be bringing anyone else?"

The lieutenant colonel shook his head. "Just us two for now."

"I look forward to it. I'll reserve parking spots right up at the front for you both. One car or two?"

"One would be fine. We're stationed on Long Island; it's not a problem. The major here has proven himself highly competent on the turnpike."

He offered a handshake. "Good afternoon, Lieutenant Colonel Baker and Major Jamison. Thank you both."

After they left, Isaac looked up. Rona was already waiting outside his door, notebook in hand.

Lunch for 4
1 parking in front
11-12:30
Confirm E Rossler

o o o

The lieutenant colonel was on the phone. "Have Lieutenant Benson get Major Jamison and I some time with General Garner on Thursday afternoon any time after 1500. Yeah, let's ask for 15 minutes. That would be great, thanks. Yes, we'll be in Princeton again that mornin' at their lab. No, they changed that. They're callin' it HELX now. Like helix, but with four letters, tha's right. Tag it as budget, okay?" Tha's all, thanks. Yeah, we're leavin' now."

"So, what did you think of Stern?" asked Major Jamison.

Baker didn't hesitate. "I think he's legit, He's got Rössler and they're doin' exactly what we've been workin' towards. And it sounds like they've got that field equation worked out."

"That's the big one right there."

"So, I think we need to get this thing movin' forward."

○ ○ ○

Isaac Stern was still at university when he first realized he had the attention of the military. A man in uniform broke from a small group touring the Bevatron facility and approached him. "I knew your father," he said. Isaac shook his hand. "My name's Williams. Sergeant Taylor Williams. We're from the AEC, at Brookhaven."

But the military had been interested in quantum field research for much longer. In fact, some of their earlier experiments had yielded successful—albeit erratic—results. As early as 1947, the U.S. Atomic Energy Commission (AEC) and the military had been experimenting in secret with high energy radar and quantum fields at McChord Field in Washington state and the Brookhaven research facility in Long Island, New York. In particular, they had begun studying how quantum field theory, via the magic of elegant math, seemed to resolve issues of causality that had, till that point plagued all relativistic quantum particle theories.

Their math, however, was not quite up to their aspirations—and it wasn't for lack of trying. In some of the early experiments at McChord, they had successfully transmitted test samples of organic matter and various molecular solids *somewhere*. Unfortunately, the mathematicians couldn't tell them where. This was a problem that remained unresolved by the researchers for 83 years, until a brilliant graduate student named Susan Alice Everett from nearby Princeton University solved the equation. And it was at Isaac Stern's HELX facility a few miles away from the main Princeton Campus that Everett and the HELX team made the discovery.

Two weeks earlier

The night of the breakthrough, Erich Rössler called Isaac Stern on his private line. "We've had a major development," he said in a hushed voice. "Somewhat unexpected, but I'm sure you'll be pleased. I've got the code here. Get a copy into safekeeping. This is definitely patentable, but you might want to have it classified as top secret instead. I'll explain more in person."

○ ○ ○

"Thanks for taking the time to meet today, Susan," said Erich. "I know you're very busy right now."

"Yeah, we're busy trying to figure out exactly which variables are responsible for the displacement effect," said Susan with a smile. "But it's very gratifying to be able to work with your team. They're really great," she said.

Erich smiled graciously. "So," he said, "I won't take too much of your time. I just want to know a little more about how you came up with this big breakthrough, really. Can you tell me *how* you came up with this brilliant equation?"

Susan shrugged. "Well, I had been thinking about the notion that time was dimensional 'like space.' And this got me thinking, you know, space is not one-dimensional. So why does almost every paper on General Relativity begin with something like 'assume a four-dimensional manifold M and a metric g.' You know, people always talk about the arrow of time, or the proverbial time *line*, yet, we talk about the union of space and time, so I began wondering why time always get reduced to a single dimension as soon as we start talking about it in physics?"

Erich had a pen in his hand but wasn't writing anything. "Interesting way of looking at it."

"So," Susan continued, "I was working with some equations based on the golden ratio spiral and the inverse of the fine structure constant, to describe how electromagnetic radiation affects charged particles."

"Planck's constant? I see...."

"I began entertaining the rather literal interpretation of what Einstein was saying, that it was dimensional *like space*—in other words, multidimensional. But, to make a long story short, it turned out that three-dimensional time provided an unexpectedly novel solution to the equation— the crux of electromagnetism, relativity, and quantum theory. And I guess that makes sense, given the way we think of time's arrow and the second law of thermodynamics and all that."

"*The total entropy of a closed system cannot decrease over time*. Yes, your equation provides a rather elegant solution for that."

"Yeah, positive entropy only. So, no traveling back in time, I guess."

"Why the golden ratio?"

"Well, as it turns out, there is a rather remarkable mathematical relationship between electromagnetism in the form of the charge of the electron, relativity in the form of the speed of light, and quantum mechanics in the form of

Planck's constant. It's this pure dimensionless number—a prime number, in fact. So, I started there."

Just then, Erich's phone buzzed. It was a terse message from Isaac.

Need you in my office ASAP.

"Come in, come in," said Isaac when Erich knocked on the door of his office. "Come on in and close the door." Isaac gestured to a chair. "Great news," he said as Erich sat down. "We've got a meeting lined up for Thursday with some folks from the government and I need you to do a demo around 11 o'clock. Just a short demo, twenty minutes, max. Can you make that happen?"

Erich was uncharacteristically serious. He didn't even pretend to be pleased by such 'great news.'

"May I ask how the government even knows about this top-secret project?" he asked bluntly.

"Erich, I appreciate your concern for maintaining the secrecy and integrity of this project, I really do, and believe me, I share your desire to ensure that we protect our intellectual property here, but I can assure you that we are not going to give away the farm here. The board and I are simply looking at licensing our tech to the government. This is not a sellout, and there will be no government project leads coming on board here in the foreseeable future. If, however, we can demonstrate that 17-second thing we did here last month—well, I think it'll knock 'em out. If we play this right, we'll be very, very well positioned for future growth in your department."

Erich felt a growing sense of anger that an answer apparently wasn't forthcoming as Isaac continued.

"So, can you demonstrate it for us on Thursday morning at 11:15 a.m.?"

"Before I answer that, please, I need to know: how do *they* know about this project?"

"Well, Erich, our patent people are already on top of the situation, and our legal team is fully engaged. We have non-disclosure agreements, the board approves. And *you* have led the team to a breakthrough success. What exactly is your concern?"

"Do these people have top-secret clearance?"

Stern responded with more certainty that he was actually sure of. "They do not. And frankly, it's irrelevant for a demonstration of this nature. We're exposing nothing but a little magic act, designed to stimulate their interest. Now, you just have to trust me on this, Erich. I need you to pull together this demo for Thursday, at 11:15 a.m. sharp. Can you do that?"

Erich gritted his teeth. "Yes, we can demonstrate on Thursday, but I really recommend top-secret clearance only."

Stern knew officers of their rank were almost certain to lack top-secret clearance. "I'll take that under advisement. Can you have a trial run ready by 9 a.m. Thursday morning to make sure everything runs smoothly?"

"Yes."

"Great. I know you'll knock 'em dead with this. Good luck."

After the meeting, Erich sat quietly in his office for a while to cool down. But his concerns nagged at him. He knew how these demos can go. He dreaded the idea of going down in history like the guy at Xerox who showed a young Steve Jobs and his Apple engineers a graphical user interface and a computer mouse back in the day. Everyone knows how that one turned out. Also, the press would certainly have a field day with this if they found out. He'd be in an article with pictures of Doc Brown and Marty McFly somewhere and *he'd* be the laughingstock, not Stern.

The long hours and late nights were hard enough. Hard on his marriage and hard on his health. In addition to running the entire lab, including the ops department, the hardware engineering group *and* the AI dev team, now he was expected to recruit a scientific brain trust to bolster the company's reputation. He'd already signed Advisory Board deals with Professor Richard Rutherford and Dr. Eldon Johnson, but Stern wanted more. Always more.

"See if Rutherford has any top-flight students in math and field theory," he suggested. "Hell, pitch it to Johnson, too. Tell 'em both we're hiring PhDs and there's a bonus for whoever gets us the right candidate."

"I will, but I really need some more support staff."

"What do you need, specifically?"

"I could use an assistant—somebody currently working on a physics degree at the university. I need somebody who can put together reports and presentations—that sort of thing. Maybe an intern."

"Sounds doable. We don't have to pay for interns, do we?"

"Ya, we should. It won't be a lot. And maybe one more. Someone young, who wants to learn the kinds of things my office is responsible for."

"What about *my* kid? He's a bit green behind the ears, but he's a good worker."

"Yeah, I'm sure he'll be fine."

"I'll talk to him when I get home tonight."

4

Solitudes of Skyscrapers

Andrew checked the time again. He tested his HELX-branded ballpoint pen and flipped to a clean sheet of paper in his notepad. It was his first day on the job at HELX—a chance to reconnect with his dad and get paid pretty well at the same time.

He looked at all the meeting notifications that had appeared in his calendar that morning. Weekly team meetings, biweekly one-on-one sessions with the team manager and monthly entries labeled as "skip level" in the executive office. Andrew had a decent office and the plum title of 'data scientist,' but didn't have a well-defined set of expectations for how or when to meet with the CEO. These regularly scheduled meetings with his father made it a lot easier.

He walked down the third-floor hall and waited at the office administrator's desk. "You can go in," she said. "He's expecting you."

"Andrew—good to see you," Isaac said in his gruff tone as

he got up from his desk. He gestured at the chairs. "Have a seat. Can I get you anything?"

"No, thanks. It's great to be here. I love my office."

"Good, good. Say, Andrew. Have you got everything you need? I know that first days in new positions often have snags."

"HR's been really helpful. Everything seems good."

"How's your mother?"

"Eh, she was not being very cool. Ever since your job offer."

"Ah, that doesn't surprise me."

"She's doing all right, though. She's got two cats now."

"And you like the job?"

"Great. I think I can really help you crunch those numbers to help improve efficiencies around here."

"Yeah, don't worry about that too much. We're on the government tit most of the time, if you know what I mean."

"Anyway, my manager says she'll be happy to have some decent analytics."

"Good, good. Andrew, ah, what do you know about what we do around here?"

"Well, I haven't been down on the lab floor yet, but I guess I know a fair amount about the equipment down there."

"Oh, you do? That's good. You know that not all of it is known to the public—those are strict rules, y'understand?"

"We've got some defense contracts and whatnot that we'd just as soon keep under our hats, so that's very important."

"I completely understand. No problem."

"Are you interested in putting some of that data science

aptitude of yours into a few of these, uh, bigger projects we have on the go here?"

"Sure, definitely."

"I'll see that you get added to the appropriate groups. They'll get y'all fixed up."

∘ ∘ ∘

By the afternoon of the next day, Andrew's security clearance had been upgraded and his manager Claudine gave him a tour of the lab floor and the special projects development office. By far the most interesting looking project he saw there was something called the Bubblecraft—technically, an exotic MHD (magnetohydrodynamic) Slipstream Accelerator—and Andrew was delighted when Claudine said this was the one he would be starting on.

Figure 1: Rendering of the first
Bubblecraft prototype, model x1

The tests started off well enough. They sent minerals, alloys, atmospheric samples, radioactive samples, plants and

—eventually—small lab animals through the system and carefully analyzed the results. And Andrew was among the VIP guests invited to show off the system when it was at last time to present it in action to the military brass.

On the morning of the day of the presentation, Andrew and the others met with the team leaders to review the game plan. They would start with a presentation and then finish up by running through the demonstrations. First, they were going to send a (rather larger than it needed to be) container carrying Plutonium-241 and Uranium-232 radioactive isotopes 80 years into the future as a dramatization of how the system could be used to solve half-life decay issues. And then, the plan was to move the Bubblecraft onto the platform (where it *had* to be—the model of the craft was a non-functional mockup, although they didn't tell the generals that) and have the craft jump forward 30 seconds in time. It would disappear and—pause for dramatic effect—then it would reappear again. *Ta-da!*

They had dressed up a mannequin in combat garb and had it sitting behind the controls of the Bubblecraft. Andrew's duties were small ones: he was in charge of making sure the mannequin looked good, and that the isotope sample was positioned with the label on the container facing the generals. The plan was to send the canister first, and finish up with the more impressive Bubblecraft stunt. For the trial run, they were using an empty mockup of the isotope canister.

Figure 2: Bubblecraft prototype x1.5 with
frame-mounted controls

"Okay," announced Claudine's voice over the loudspeaker. "Ready for the canister test. Sending in 3... 2..." Andrew reached over to adjust the position on the isotope jar....

"No, don't put your hand th... *oh*."

A split-second later the container disappeared and Andrew's right hand instantly became old and wrinkled.

"Don't *ever* put your hand inside the field while the system is operating." Andrew was rubbing his wrist. "Are you all right? Oh *dear*. We'd better get that looked at."

o o o

Although the dev team did not yet have a fully mobile Bubblecraft prototype (or even complete mathematical models to support all of their projections), this did not stop them from producing detailed sample scenarios depicting various hoped-for experimental outcomes. The calculations that predicted the most interesting results were those in which Boolean math operations such as AND, OR, NOT, and XOR yielded novel interactions between multiple Alcubierre bubble fields. They told the military that, via the use of these mathematical operations on the quantum wavefunctions of both a time displacement platform and a smaller Bubblecraft on that platform, they expected to be able to create a "field within a field"—essentially creating an Alcubierre bubble on the platform and another on the craft simultaneously. Then, by running Boolean operations on the two fields, they would be able to create a time-jump scenario where accelerated time displacement effects would occur only within the inner or outer bubble.

The pitch deck they showed to the military brass highlighted several possible uses for this type of capability:

- Accelerated healing
- Rapid growth of cloned subjects
- Accelerated food production
- Threat disposal
- Collateral damage deferral
- Optional drone mode reconnaissance system

One example scenario rather fancifully depicted a chrononaut traveling into the future without experiencing accelerated aging, while bringing along rapidly grown food. Another showed how the system could simplify the handling of hazardous radioactive waste by simply by sending it as far into the future as required.

Figure 3: Bubblecraft x2 with safety ring-based controls

"This," Erich Rössler explained to his guests, "is our second-generation design. The first-gen field accelerator used a two-dimensional time variable. We've since found that my wrapping that 5-D space with an additional dimensional variable, which we're currently calling 'perceived time', we end up with a full 1-to-1 match between the dimensionality of time and space. We call that 'time-space,' to distinguish it from the common Einsteinian terminology of space-time. By adding that third dimension—which was completely out of the scope of that first-gen accelerator design—we can uncouple the effect from a specific location. And that's how we came up with the Bubblecraft idea. In essence, we took that 2.5-D toroidal field and made a three-dimensional bubble out of it. Now we can move that bubble almost anywhere we want, as long as we've got the power to run the thing."

It was a classic proof-of-concept tech demo. The capabilities they showed barely worked, and the things they only talked about didn't work at all. But the demo did the trick, and a few weeks later, Isaac Stern successfully negotiated a deal with the U.S. Department of Defense for delivery of a working second-gen Bubblecraft device for $33.4 billion. It was, at the time, the most expensive single project ever funded by the DOD's science and technology (S&T) budget.

o o o

When it finally got into their hands, the military folks had their own ideas on how to use the technology. Most significantly, the Alcubierre Bubblecraft made an ideal stealth attack vehicle. It could appear in a location, drop off packages or personnel, and then disappear right on out of there, just like that.

Its vehicle-mounted field generator allowed field deployments virtually anywhere. In fact, early field tests conducted around the New Mexico area led to a few accidents, when incoming test packages intersected wildlife or other transient occupants of the same space-time coordinates.

To help offset this risk, they asked the HELX team to develop a solution that would transmit an "incoming" warning message slightly ahead of the primary deliverable. The newly submitted requirements doc also listed the ability to control the jump-length or even initiate additional jumps from within the Bubblecraft itself.

○ ○ ○

The possibility of sending a message or even a molecular payload to a destination without an established receiving station opened up a number of intriguing possibilities. First of all, it would allow a truly mobile solution that could be applied to vehicular systems of almost any type—even spacecraft. And then there was the potential for sending schematics ahead that would allow those at the destination to build a 'quantum communications' device that would allow two-way communications between the two time periods.

This capability was potentially far more valuable than simple one-way messaging, but the HELX team couldn't seem to crack the problem. The concept seemed relatively straightforward, as least as straightforward as things get in the world of entangled qubits and spooky action at a distance. But even after three years of effort to develop a working implementation, the sender never heard a ping back from the receiver. That was until NASA got involved.

George Gunderson, who was the HELX engineer primarily responsible for the toroidal field technology the Bubblecraft used, knew some of the engineers at the Houston Space Center and, through them, found out the names of some of the officials that were interested in this sort of research.

"Doing preliminary development work on quantum communications through temporal displacement fields, would like to discuss," was the tantalizing text of the email George sent.

Later that week, he received a call back from an extremely enthusiastic project manager. "Good day, Mister Gunderson. My name is Alan Hull," the man said. "I manage a group of people at NASA working on something that sounds quite similar. We'd like to meet with you to discuss your work and, you know, compare notes."

"That sounds great," said George. A meeting was set for 10 a.m. the following Tuesday. As it turned out, this group at NASA had already been approached by Isaac Stern and had at least a rudimentary understanding of the HELX team's early successes in temporal displacement.

"I understand you were on the team that did that first 17-second jump?"

"Well, that's officially considered top secret. But seeing as how I didn't tell you about it, I think it's safe to say 'yes.'"

"You must know the folks from Cornerstone, then." Alan Hull certainly knew a lot of what George had always been told was top-secret stuff.

"I do—not especially well, but, yes, we've met."

"Well, look George," said Alan after he reviewed George's notes, "I can tell you that we've already tested and discarded the method you describe here. We spent months trying to get it working—at this point, we just don't think it works that way at all. The problem with that method is an issue our guys and gals tell me is called the no-communication theorem. So, we've been working on some possible workarounds. One that we are just starting to test right now is showing some promise, however. As you may know, quantum teleportation is a technique for transferring quantum information from a sender at one location to a receiver some distance away. We think that by implementing quantum teleportation with a distance of zero, we can utilize a classical information channel to transmit quantum information. We're using both resources to achieve what is impossible for either alone."

"That is brilliant," said George. "I think you might be onto something there."

o o o

"I want you to promise me something," Isaac said to Andrew during their monthly meeting. "Someday, this property —the land this facility is built upon—will be yours. I want you to promise that you'll never sell the land. Go ahead and lease it if you want, but don't sell it under any circumstances —and don't let ex-wives take it away from you. It's a family heirloom, and we've always promised to keep it in the family. Y'understand?"

As he was telling this to Andrew, Isaac remembered when

his own father had said something similar to him. And as Andrew watched and listened to his father, he wondered if he would someday be sitting in that chair, giving this speech to his own young son or daughter. None of Andrew's female friends were serious prospects for the title of Mrs. Andrew Stern. Not yet, anyway.

Andrew nodded, but his father's voice was all but drowned out by his internal thoughts. His mother had been so unhappy to learn that her husband was soliciting military contracts. He was practically an arms dealer. And he wasn't even supposed to tell her about it.

"Y'understand?"

"I promise," vowed Andrew.

Isaac closed the Day Timer binder on his desk and stood up. "All right. Well, good to see you."

"Thank you, sir."

o o o

"All he talks about is his work," Marcie complained to her best friend Amelia over lunch, "and he is *so* defensive and sometimes openly critical of any suggestions that he take a break from whatever problem he's obsessing about at the time. He *ignores* my pals when they ask him to take part in whatever *they're* doing."

Amelia took a sip of diet cola and looked her in the eye. "Look," she confided, "I know he's got money and he's kinda good lookin' but honey, you must have noticed. Most of our friends avoid him at this point and, honestly, I can understand why. He's getting kind of scary."

Marcie picked at her salad glumly. "I mean, yeah, I guess he's got what you might call leadership skills and business sense and all that, but it's kinda creepy the way he goes on about Objectivism, you know? Like the other day, when he was *lecturing* me about how reason is his only absolute. It's a pretty strident moral philosophy. He keeps talking about how his own happiness is the moral purpose of his life—and 'to thine own self be true.'"

"What about *your* happiness, darlin'?" said Amelia, pondering her own fingernails.

"I know! The way he says it sometimes, it just sounds so selfish."

"Pompous," proclaimed Amelia. "Frankly, I couldn't put up with him."

o o o

5

Reorg

2036

The news of the all-hands meeting came out of the blue, as these things often do. One moment, the team was executing on a well-thought-out strategic vision and the next... well, here's a brand-new plan from the folks upstairs. Resources were repurposed and budgets re-allocated. Entire teams were laid off as strategic and marketing pillars were re-aligned. Vision documents and mission statements had to be rewritten, with new logos and letterheads. And, invariably, a few heads had to roll.

There had been rumors for weeks that a reorg was in the works, but few expected it to be as much of a shakeup as it now appeared. It was always hard to tell how 'significant' a reorg would end up looking a couple of years after the fact. Most of them ended up being nothing more than a lot of buzzwords and empty promises, but this one felt like something more pivotal.

This was certainly not the usual iterative model that some of the old-timers had been predicting. Far from it. This was like throwing out the baby with the bathwater and then throwing out the tub as well. Not only was the company name, brand identity, and mission statement changing, so was the entire board of directors. But this time, they weren't being replaced by newcomers. They were being replaced by an AI arbiter. Resources would be re-allocated dynamically; managed via the blockchain. And the man responsible for instigating this change was Isaac Stern.

Today's all-hands meeting was, in Stern's words, a repositioning for the future. The company was pivoting from its original emphasis in particle accelerators and leaning into what he claimed was summed up in their new tagline: "New Worlds. Beyond."

"By bringing our world-class blockchain security and rich application and automation services portfolio for improving performance, availability, and management together with our industry-leading software application delivery and API management solutions, unparalleled credibility and brand recognition in the DevOps community, and massive user base, we bridge the divide between NetOps and DevOps with A.I.-enabled application automation services and enterprise-class multi-cloud environments," he said, in an announcement that was widely covered by both the tech press and financial market reporters.

Stern's claims that the company would "integrate our cloud-native quantum blockchain technology with state-of-the-art deep learning software and load balancing A.I.

technology to create a more holistic brand identity as a leading name in cutting-edge research and development" made front-page news in markets around the world.

Some market watchers claimed it was just another set of empty buzzwords from a company desperate to stay relevant in an uncertain market; others opined that that what this really meant was that the research dollars had all but dried up in the high-energy particle accelerator research field where institutional investors, governments, and business partners no longer saw an acceptable return on their considerable investments. These days, claimed the pundits, CERN was the only brand with name recognition worthy of that research community's attention. All the big money was now flowing in the direction of A.I. research and quantum field theory.

"Despite our best efforts," Stern told the financial news reporters at the press conference that day, "retaining top talent in this country was becoming a problem with our old mission statement."

One of the other things that was changing was the company's brand identity—again. Before it had been dissolved, the outgoing board of directors had been discussing possible replacements for "HELX," which was now viewed as too limited and unimaginative for a company as dynamic and diverse as this one now was.

The name HELX, they argued, still sounded too heavily focused on the old paradigms of collider research: high-energy particle acceleration wasn't as investor-friendly as AI and quantum blockchain. And besides, they weren't even using a large accelerator anymore, so the acronym didn't even apply.

Apparently, the AI agreed. When posed the question of how the company should be branded to best represent its diverse portfolio, the analytics engine's executive output module responded by saying: "We need a more exciting and diversified brand identity that suggests bold experimentation, AI and deep learning expertise, and new frontiers in virtual reality—attributes that reflect a positive future for humanity itself." And so HELX was out and a new name was chosen: XAVR.

Meant to be pronounced as "Xavier," the announcement of the new name was accompanied by a computer-generated avatar meant to personify the AI-based entity, and the image and name quickly became a meme, with the image of XAVR's "face" inserted anywhere a public figure seemed to be acting as an agent of shallow corporatism. Erotic fanfiction paired XAVR with everyone from Mister Spock to the J.R. 'Bob' Dobbs character from the Church of the SubGenius.

In fact, it had been Isaac's son, Andrew, who had suggested a more human-centered name—something that suggested scientific research, humanism, and reflected the company's widening palette of interests in areas for potential future diversification.

○ ○ ○

The AI-based management module had stack-ranked employees and executives by job criticality, performance ratings and something it called an innovation index, decreasing the overall head count by 15 percent that first year. The stock market responded by increasing the company's valuation in kind. All hiring and promotion was automated to maximize disruptive potential. New hires and new levels of responsibility matched the keywords and performance attributes described by aspirational goals, not skill sets. Those unwilling to take big risks, fail fast, and pivot often were quickly removed. The pace of change was dizzying. "This," the pundits crowed, "is how all businesses will be managed in the next decade."

"Freactive resource management," the latest press release called it. Isaac's business manager, Rona Wells, fumed as she read about this all-new, AI-led *strategic* approach to what the company touted as "freer" enterprise. "The goddamned press release reads like it was *written* by a bot, for Chrissake," she complained. (It was.)

It was little more than a marketing slogan at launch, but the "freactive" jargon, wrapped in promises of a truly intelligent org that would do away with the need for old-fashioned decision making, appealed to those particularly starry-eyed investors that had seen their wildest financial dreams come true in the form of HELX/XAVR stock valuations.

Indeed, the highest valuation in the company's history occurred just after the HELX-to-XAVR transition. The growth peaked two weeks before the company announced what it called its biggest breakthrough ever: Exosentience. This, the press release gushed, was their patented technology that would, for the first time ever, deliver a better-than-human level of machine sentience.

Old-fashioned decision making was obsolete, it boasted, and so was Isaac Stern's role as CEO. The management module, having already done away with the board, now decided that Isaac was redundant.

Rona was in a business development meeting in Isaac's office when two flunkies from the building security department had—apparently on orders from what she disparagingly referred to as 'the big mac' itself—ordered him to be removed from the building. Into his executive office they marched and he was escorted out, past the astonished gaze of his executive assistant and the others in the leadership office. A young woman Isaac didn't know held up her camera phone.

"Don't you dare," he warned.

Rona punched a button on the phone. "Get my car to the front door. Now."

o o o

In happier days, Rona Wells had worked as a business development manager in the AI and Deep Learning Research Division. Her team had achieved some acclaim under her leadership and Isaac, on the rebound from the failure of his first marriage, had taken notice of her. She shared his enthusiasm for piquing investor interest by emphasizing the FOMO[1] factor—and for the most part, it worked.

---

[1] Fear of missing out

The stock market had responded favorably to the buzz-word-rich news of the company's focus on AI. As the old HELX signs on the building were replaced by the new XAVR brandmarks, the believers hyped the stock on the investment forums and the market movers rode the stock up at a rapid rate. The potential, brokers said, was practically limitless. Rona and Isaac's office romance rode on this wave of investor optimism and she moved in with him four months later.

But just nine weeks after that, a consortium backed by two majors was making headlines and rumors of a trans-flash ban spooked investors and the stock value stumbled. Then, a group of disgruntled hedge-fund managers launched a lawsuit against Isaac. As CEO of MPAX and HELX, Isaac had protected himself from personal liability claims; now, the perception that XAVR was in charge made it more difficult.

At 6:10 in the morning, Isaac was still asleep. Rona cast a glance at the alarm clock and lay on her side, thinking about how much value the company had shed in the past 48 hours. She felt less certain about Isaac's ability to weather this flash-forward controversy. There was too much to lose for her to ignore. She urged Isaac to go all-in with a fiduciary negligence complaint that argued in favor of turning off the AI's higher functioning sentience and reclaiming his role as CEO.

It may have seemed an ideal investment platform for players in the long-term markets for everything from bonds and mortgages to microtransactions, but it was always about the long game. Now, that game was rigged, and Isaac was convinced that a lawsuit—for $35.2 billion in calculated losses, no less—was an even better bet in the long game.

Isaac had been made something of a meme-worthy laughing stock at the end of the previous fiscal year when the machine intelligence algorithm he approved and funded unceremoniously terminated his positions as CEO and chairman of the corporation. And now, less than a year after it had launched, that algorithm had come up what the pundits were calling the ultimate long game. And he—the AI's only real competition—was the first executive role to be re-allocated to big mac, the big machine. The debacle appeared on several of the tech press' Best/Worst of the Decade lists.

Suddenly, XAVR announced that it was filing for Chapter 11 bankruptcy protection—and that it was acting as its own legal team. Three months later, rumors began to circulate that it had been bailed out by the government, with a new pro-military mandate. The languishing stock price made a partial comeback amid the reports of both the investors' grievances, and Stern's own lawsuit against the company.

What of the plan, the investors' attorneys argued, to take XAVR's AI global and deliver multinational and governmental editions? What about the AI-led CRISPR8 work in the bioengineering space? These initiatives had resulted in solid gains in the previous year. Suddenly, those high-performing projects are on hold and we are supposed to believe in jump bonds?

Although the company's time-travel tech was top secret, it was well known that huge military contracts had been signed. The management module played an expert game of buzzword bingo in its press releases, allowing speculation to push the stock price ever higher.

Internally, too, the AI was calculating the odds to maximize long-term gains.

Although XAVR's press releases often touted various benefits of the company's ever-increasing scale of computational prowess, its actions often didn't match the claims. It dumbed down its business AI services to make them easier to use; it restricted business activities and resources so that it only did business with the companies that were interested in its most profitable services. End-user products were discontinued in favor of subscription-only enterprise-exclusive services. Anything that didn't match the management module's ever-changing area of focus was discontinued.

The AI apparently took a dim view of the value of long-term holdings of almost anything that wasn't real estate or what it termed 'classic collectibles'—a catch-all category that included art, classic cars, and other rare and precious items.

But many of these items, even, seemed to have a 'best before' date. The AI tended to take a dim view of such prospects in the far-distant future where, perhaps, the odds of natural disasters or other calamities made investments in these ephemeral arts less viable.

In terms of big bets, the AI executive was all in on bioengineering and genetic research and, of course, "business AI" in general. Somewhat surprisingly, it seemed less bullish on the commercial potential for the company's proprietary temporal displacement technology, despite the military's enthusiasm for it.

As the AI executive plotted out its plans for commercializing the time-travel tech, it spun off subroutines dedicated to solving any problems it anticipated. Chief among these was the fact that its military and U.S. government partners held exclusive rights to some of the key time-travel technologies.

So, the AI set about reverse-engineering its own code as a clean-room design. This was practical primarily due to the fact that the top-secret nature of the code licensed to the military had never been publicly disclosed through patent filings. The 'Chinese wall' approach of clean-room design would, it predicted, protect the company against copyright claims.

At the same time, the management module began buying land and component production facilities in what it determined would be ideal locations for commercial jump-stations. Affluent high-tech urban centers with key infrastructure components, major ports, a suitable workforce, and facilities with synergistic elements rose to the top of the dynamic list.

After a brief period in which a Silicon Valley presence topped the candidate list, it fell in the rankings—apparently due to labor and land costs—and Seattle, Washington and Houston, Texas made the top two spots in the final list.

As the AI began buying land in and around these areas, the management module began investing in companies in strategically related industries, betting on leaks and rumors to fill in the gaps in speculators' imaginations.

It invested in bioengineering, robotics and automation systems, additive manufacturing, on-demand services, international shipping and logistics, quantum computing, and more.

Speculators wondered what it all meant.

It was predicted that the commercial market for "temporal transportation" market would soon outpace the scientific and research uses already booked solid for the next four years. New jump-stations would have to be built to serve all these predicted use cases. Projections forecast millions of users in the coming decade. Optimists saw the potential for reductions in social costs; pessimists foresaw the erosion of the workforce.

This was all speculative, of course. There were no commercial customers yet. But the market seemed sure that would soon change.

Then something unexpected happened. It deemphasized investments in the temporal tech and other non-public areas of development.

As soon as the focus shifted away from the its proven moneymakers, the wild stock ride ended. Now the pundits complained about core markets being ignored. The AI had failed, cried the Chicken Littles, and Isaac was one of the expendables.

"Idiots," mumbled Isaac. Rona sighed and picked up his empty coffee cup as he reviewed yesterday's disastrous financial results.

"It's time to go."

○ ○ ○

Welcome to your debt-free future, the poster at the lawyer's office said. Rona sat silently with Isaac as they waited for the doors to open.

Inside the office, his lawyer laid it all out: Contingent

stakeholders had filed lawsuits against him, despite the fact that XAVR had been in control; legal arguments focused on neglect of fiduciary duty in allowing XAVR to assume control in the first place. Another filing cited the supposed abandonment of the company's cash-cow genetics cloud as further proof of willful neglect of stakeholder interests. Suddenly, computing time was unavailable, the suits alleged—and it was true, but the company couldn't reveal the real reason—a massive chunk of XAVR's processing power was going into the top-secret temporal displacement project. Work on the big-ticket items in the portfolio work was said to be a priority, but the results suggested otherwise. The stock was vulnerable and investor-led litigants hollered on social media, demanding reparations, if not blood.

And so, Isaac Stern, former interim director, chairman and CEO of the company formerly known as the quantum physics research lab at Princeton University was the man the press focused their attention on as the victim of his own technological weaponry—the man they had lauded only a year earlier for boldly transforming this fledgling company from an academic research facility into a money-making investor magnet was now viewed as a man without a future.

The AI had, of course, responded dynamically to these changing conditions—it countered with moves both political and economic. In this suddenly challenged economic climate, the business system's strategic and marketing pillars were re-aligned. Vision documents and mission statements were rewritten yet again. And, this time, the AI itself threw Isaac

Stern under the bus, blaming the former CEO for the mess the company now found itself in.

The newly AI-led company announced another massive wave of layoffs as part of what it characterized as its ongoing strategic growth and market positioning plan. The stock value regained some of its lost ground on new predictions of next-quarter dividends.

In the words of the company's newly appointed "virtual" chairman and chief executive authority—dubbed the "vCEO" —today's all-hands meeting was "a repositioning for the future in response to rapidly changing market conditions."

"We will exploit our technology's ability to rapidly adapt to achieve and maintain a market-leading advantage in A.I. technologies by spinning off the XAVR name as our exclusive brand of AI-based business assistance services," it said. "We are proud to announce our new *unified* corporate brand identity as Andna LLC, now *the* leading name in cutting-edge research and development."

o o o

Did you know?

80% of businesses around the world have been successful when their brand names end with a vowel sound.

6

Aftermath

2037

"Andrew, I'm afraid we won't be having any more of these monthly meetings. Y'see, the company put its artificial intelligence technology in charge and it has, uh, eliminated my position. Yeah, can't be helped. So... good luck. Keep in touch."

Suddenly Isaac just looked like a sad old man. They both sat there in silence for a moment.

"Wait, why did they did they do that?"

"Oh, they're all gaga over this thing called a DAO—a decentralized autonomous organization. It runs on an AI engine and maintains a blockchain-based ledger. Anyway, recent instabilities in the tech sector have really stung them and I'm taking the fall. It's a tough game sometimes."

"And, I'm sorry to say, they've given you and everyone else in Claudine's department your two-week notice as well. And Rona, too. She's leaving with me. We're going to get married."

So much to unpackage. "Wow, congrats, I guess."

Andrew looked at his father, but Isaac avoided his gaze and busied himself by straightening his desk organizer and pens.

"So, two weeks?"

Yeah, you can take your holidays now if you have any accrued."

"Yes, I do. Well, is there anything I can help you with, dad?"

"No no, gosh no. I'll be fine. I'll be keeping the Bentley. Not sure about the house. But we'll be fine."

Exiled to his home office, Andrew's unhappiness spilled over into his personal life. His girlfriend Marcie left him, and he felt frustrated by his inability to continue his work. With his high-security clearance set to run out in a few days, he dictated a message to his friend George into his phone. He decided against using the office mail system and sent it privately via a VPN.

I need to meet with you today or tomorrow. Please get in touch ASAP.

George agreed to meet with Andrew that evening after work. They met, as they often did, at the local bar. When Andrew arrived, George had already ordered him a beer. "You sounded as though you might enjoy a beer. It's on me. So, what's going on?"

"Thanks," Andrew said as he tipped glasses with his friend. He explained the situation with his father and his security clearance and they discussed their respective futures. On the TV just behind them, a news item scrolled by below a picture of the Andna Building. "Replaced by Blockchain, Ex-CEO Stern sues Andna."

"Hey look," said George, pointing to the TV. Two talking heads were speaking and the graphic behind them showed a picture of Isaac Stern and a graph of the plummeting stock value. The closed captions told the story. "Thursday afternoon, the stock of Andna Corporation plummeted 24.2 percent on yet another scandal, following last week's ousting of Chairman and CEO Isaac Stern. In the latest incident, a government contract worth an estimated $32.4 billion dollars was canceled today, following the layoff of more than 700 employees at the beleaguered company's Princeton-based headquarters. Andna Corporation made news last month when a pair of high-ranking officials were convicted of fraud and tax evasion charges and sentenced to 7 years in federal prison."

As George and Andrew watched the TV coverage of the debacle, George frowned and shook his head. "There's a lot more to it than what they're saying," he said. He noted that prior to the removal of Isaac Stern, the board of directors had approved a trial of becoming an A.I.-led decentralized autonomous organization. The A.I. proposed various motions, one of which was to allow the *'management'* algorithm to run without explicit board interference. "Once it had their approval for that," he explained, "the first thing it did was eliminate the board, followed by the CEO position itself. The board should never have allowed that level of autonomy, but I suppose they didn't foresee an action that was so Draconian."

The two executives convicted of fraud and tax evasion leveled similar charges, insisting that switching to an AI-based "vCEO" was never intended to be a permanent solution without the possibility of change. The AI, they alleged, was deliberately exposing damaging information, then buying back huge blocks of stock to drive the price back up.

"It's the natural end-result of a fully autonomous system designed by and for MBAs," marveled George. "It's completely ruthless, and will do whatever it takes to drive gains in its stock value. Remarkable, really."

"Yes, but none of that is new. Isn't that what every CEO tries to do?"

"Sure, but the combination of the system's ruthless directives and the sheer speed at which these market maneuvers are being undertaken is the innovation."

"It's maintaining a level of activity that yields a cash-positive result, while consistently strengthening its position. Based on changing conditions, it continuously recalculates the solution with the greatest likelihood of resulting in a net-positive outcome."

"Because the system is fully heuristic," George theorized, "it has learned the fastest way to add value is to drive the price down, buy, then pump the stock back up and sell high."

"Well, it's not working very well today. The stock is down 24 percent."

"Yes, but that was primarily the result of the cancellation of that big government contract. If you look historically, every big drop has been followed by subsequent gains. And I'm sure that right now, it's doing whatever it can to compensate for this unexpected new condition—probably by buying a shit-ton of stock back at bargain-basement prices."

He pulled out his phone and looked at a graph of the latest Andna stock activity. "See? Huge blocks purchased a few minutes ago and already the share price is up almost 15 percent."

He logged into the Andna network. "XAVR, show management module activity over the last 10 minutes," he commanded.

He pushed the phone toward Andrew and pointed to the display terminal output. "See here? As the algorithm proceeds, the system takes various actions: hire, fire, invest, divest, and so on. The novel feature is *management*'s ability to self-write and execute custom programs to interact with opportunities as they arise."

"Management recommends a campaign to reposition publicity over Stern lawsuit," said XAVR.

"Show activity over the last 48 hours" commanded George.

'Board dissolves, citing complete confidence in AI leadership,' suggested the AI.

"All right, that's enough," said George as he closed the app and the system was silenced.

Andrew ran his left index finger around the rim of his beer glass. As usual, a glove covered his right hand. "I have a question for you on another topic," he said.

"Shoot," replied George.

"As far as I can tell, the way the Bubblecraft works, the field effect is managed via an service called the Lagrangian Output Wavefunction Cloud, yes?"

"That's right. We call it the 'Low Cloud.'"

"And it runs on the Bubblecraft's onboard computer, right?"

"It pretty much has to," said George. "We can't have it

running on an external cloud service because, as soon as we jump forward, the service wouldn't be there anymore. We have to bring it forward with us. That's the main difference from the old HELX design, where the platform stayed put. There, we relied on the cloud services supplied by the main AI, so we could start or stop it, and we could see the user logs and so on. That system wouldn't run at all, of course, if the cloud was turned off, so that was the main problem we had to solve," he said with a smile.

"And you did that by having the A.I. generate a smaller, more portable version of itself?"

"More or less. It was essentially a quantized version of the larger module, running on a highly optimized onboard firmware platform. We can still connect to the full learning set in the cloud to get updates and whatnot, but otherwise it runs independently. And, we haven't announced it yet, but the newest rev of the Bubblecraft will work without an external power source, too."

"It's a beautiful design, George."

"Well, it's not all by me. I just did the engineering."

Andrew finished his beer and set the glass down. "The *main* engineering. And my father holds the patent on this?"

"I know there's more than one patent—about 20, actually. He might hold those patents personally, or—I dunno, I haven't looked them up for a long time—he might have assigned them to a corporate entity of some sort to keep them out of the hands of the big machine."

"And hopefully out of the government's Top Secrets file, as well."

"I'm honestly not sure about that. There's a thing called the Invention Secrecy Act, which the U.S. government uses to keep patents deemed 'detrimental to the national security' on lockdown."

"Huh. So, if there *was* a space-based version, it wouldn't need an earth-based cloud connection."

"Right. The power requirements might be a problem on a spacecraft, though. They tend to go for low-power devices up there. We currently require a 220-volt power source. It stores the charge in the onboard batteries and discharges it through a set of quick-discharge capacitors. There's enough charge for about three jumps, in case there's an emergency at the initial or secondary jump points. Until the craft arrives as its destination, it's still in the life cycle of the previous bubble. We have a small onboard computer that can manage the basics. And," said George, finishing off his beer, "it can enable the optional network if it needs access to the learning set—which it usually doesn't. But the external learning set might be required if the system hit an unexpected event at the destination, say an earthquake or a catastrophe of some sort. It should theoretically even make it okay in the case of a power outage."

Andrew nodded and pulled a $20 bill from his pocket. "But what you're saying is it doesn't really need to connect to the cloud for anything other than updates."

"Right. Oh, I forgot to mention that the new Bubblecraft is also going to support onboard quantum communications via entangled status bits."

"Oh yeah. That's a great feature."

"Yeah. We don't have a patent on that. That was NASA's

idea. We were trying to do it with quantum communication, which didn't work—they had success with zero-distance quantum teleportation."

George noticed the bill in Andrew's hand. "No, keep your money, man. This one's on me."

"Thanks for the beer. Man, you should be in charge. The big machine that made the company billions, that's your idea, dude," Andrew said emphatically.

"Nah, they *spent* billions, but those Cornerstone guys walked out over a snag in the negotiations after all their big talk. That really hurt your dad's credibility."

"Hmm. Too bad," said Andrew. "Hey, how about removing a name from the user list?"

"To hide it from the jump logs, you mean? Nah, if you remove an ID from the authorization group you lose access to all the services in the group. You can rename things, though."

"Could you change my user name, keeping all of my existing security clearances and admin privileges and then make another dummy account with my old name—and set the dates on them so the changes aren't obvious?"

"Well, we're really not supposed to."

"I'll give you five thousand bucks. Cash."

"Hm. When do you want it done?"

"How 'bout now?"

He handed George an envelope. "Don't put it in the bank," he said.

o o o

At exactly 00:00:00 on July 1, a scheduled event by the

name of "scheduled cam test" was written into the Andna security logs. The cameras blinked for a fraction of a second and for the next minute, showed a static video frame with a dynamic overlay showing a fake clock readout updating every second—just as the real security feed's display did—instead of a live feed. A figure wearing a hoodie and a low-slung cap entered via an outside door and scurried past the now-inoperative camera's viewpoint. As the seconds continued to increment on the cam's fake security feed, a large dome-shaped object was wheeled into the back of the big truck. At fifty seconds past midnight, the cargo box door was rolled down, storage bay door was closed and the figure left the building.

When the clock reached 00:01:00:00, the camera feed switched back over to the live display and the truck pulled away unseen in the darkness.

o o o

7

Inside Job

"Investigators are puzzled by the disappearance of top-secret research equipment in what now appears to be an inside job at the New Jersey headquarters of beleaguered Andna Corporation. Security cameras and tracking equipment were deliberately disabled, say investigators, and efforts to discover the perpetrators of the crime have so far been unsuccessful."

"We are investigating the possibility that terrorism or at least funding by foreign nationals might be involved, and have not discounted the possibility that this is the work of disgruntled ex-employees, of which there are several hundred."

"Efforts to recover the missing equipment, which the company says is part of its top-secret research portfolio, are still underway as the investigation continues. Dorine Kwan, NNC news."

○ ○ ○

Andrew texted George. *Please call me ASAP. Urgent.*

A response came back immediately. *ok.*

A moment later, the phone rang and there was George. "Whoa. What time is it?"

"It's late. Sorry. I need some help unloading a truck," Andrew said. "I need your help, and it has to be now."

George considered telling Andrew that he had other plans —in fact, she was the reason he was still awake—but he kept quiet. "Okay, man—where are we meeting?"

"Southeast corner, one block east of my place," said Andrew.

"Okay, I'm on my way," George said. He turned to the woman in his bed, who was pouting a little. "I'll be back as soon as I can, baby, and I'll make it up to you—I promise," he told her.

"You better," she said with a wink.

Andrew had half-expected a cadre of law enforcement agents to descend upon him as soon as the Bubblecraft was reported missing, so he had rather cautiously parked the truck a block away from his house.

When George arrived, Andrew explained that they had to unload the truck at his storage facility. He didn't, however, mention that the facility was nothing more than an old double-wide garage. It was deliberately low-tech. There were no security cameras and the garage was at the back corner of his property—and completely deserted at this time of night. There was no one around when they walked down the street at the front of the house, looking there, and on the nearby side streets, for suspicious vans or other vehicles that might be part of a stakeout operation. There were none. Finally satisfied that they weren't being watched, Andrew pulled the truck around to the alley and onto the landing. George hopped out of the cab and unlocked the gate, then guided him as he backed into the driveway area in front of the garage.

He shut off the engine and jumped out into the silence of the night. He handed George a flashlight and unlocked the rear door of the truck.

Their flashlights shone into the dark interior of the cargo box. Inside was a dome-shaped object under a large tarp.

"Is that what I think it is?"

"I'm pretty sure it is," said Andrew.

"This thing's worth thirty billion fucking dollars, you beautiful madman," said George.

Andrew loosened the straps holding it in place. "Let's get it into the garage."

George and Andrew tipped the Bubblecraft onto its tiny rear rollers and wheelbarrowed it down the ramp from the truck and into the storage area of the garage. It was surprisingly light, being mostly comprised of hollow beta-titanium alloy tubing. George no longer found it hard to fathom how Andrew could have spirited it away, out of the field test storage area at Andna and into this truck.

"So, how did you manage to make off with this thing?"

"It was in the field test storage area. I just backed the truck up to the loading dock and moved it inside."

"Pretty ballsy. I thought you were just going to use the big rig. Any problems with the special security clearance I set up for you?"

"No. Everything worked just like you said it would."

"So… are you going to try to sell it?"

Andrew looked genuinely startled at the suggestion. "Oh God, no," he said. "I can't imagine the kind of people I'd have to do business with, or the risks that would entail. I just want to, you know, see the future. It's got to be better this. It's just got to."

They moved it into place inside the dark garage and Andrew picked up the tarp he had set aside for it.

"You should probably test this beast while I'm here," George suggested, "just to make sure it made the trip in one piece. If it does need fixing, it would be a shame to miss the opportunity to do so while I'm here."

"I just hate to see things go to waste," said Andrew. "And I figured that we might be able to find something to do with it. I want you to help me get it powered up. I figure the best way to hide this thing is to make it disappear for a few years… and I'm willing to go with it."

"We can't do that tonight," George cautioned. "Do we have all the cables we need?"

Andrew nodded. "I think so."

"And what about the batteries?"

"They're here in the box," Andrew assured him.

"You should probably plug the charger in. It'll take 6 hours to charge fully."

"Yeah. Good thinking." Andrew plugged it in.

"Well, look, let's lock the place up and get a good night's sleep. You're not going to disappear for God knows how long without at least letting me get a few hours rest before I have to set all this stuff up and run through all the safety checks."

"Fair enough. D'ya think it will be safe to leave this thing here overnight?"

Hard to say but if anybody's looking for you, they'll be looking for you at your house, right? So, stay at my place tonight. And move the truck."

"All right. That sounds like a plan. Thanks."

"Just don't mind me. I have a lady friend staying over."

"I'll be as quiet as a mouse."

"We probably won't."

o o o

George opened the front door of his condo and he and Andrew stepped into the foyer. George fetched a blanket and a pillow and dropped them on the couch in the living room. "These should do the trick," he said. "I'll see you in the morning. If you need anything, just help yourself."

o o o

The next morning, Andrew woke up to see an attractive young woman opening the fridge. "Hey," she said, "I'm Cleo."

"Andrew. Pleased to meet you."

George came out with a coffee. "Hey, good morning. I see you two have met."

"Yeah, just now."

She poured a glass of orange juice. "You're a friend of George's, huh?"

"Yes, we worked together."

"Andrew just got into town," George fibbed, "so I very graciously let him crash on the couch."

"That was *uncharacteristically* gracious of you," she teased.

"Just like old times, eh, Andrew?"

"I hope I didn't bother you," said Andrew.

"Same," said Cleo, amused at George's not-quite-straight face.

"Andrew's dad owns the place we work at," George explained. "I mean, he literally owns the ground it's built on."

"Wow, so you're Isaac Stern's son? He's a big deal around there. Nice to meet ya. Are you a programmer or a business type of guy?"

"I'm more of a business guy, you might say. A data scientist."

"Cleo's quite a programmer. She works on the front-end stuff for the control surfaces and all that."

"You just wanted to see my code," she teased, playfully tugging on George's t-shirt. She turned toward Andrew. "Are you staying around for the long weekend?"

"I'm not sure. Probably not. George is just helping me with a few, uh, errands."

"Hey George, is that remote account still working?"

"Should be."

Andrew pulled a laptop from his bag and booted up the system. He logged in and checked that his remote access was working as expected. As he did so, several "new mail" notification pings were heard. Andrew ignored them.

George, meanwhile, was looking at his phone—intently at

first, then with an alarmed expression. "Oh my god," he said in a hushed voice.

Cleo entered the bathroom and closed the door. George walked closer to Andrew and lowered his voice a little. "So, I have some bad news, I'm afraid. It's pretty bad, man—you might want to sit down."

"Yeah, no doubt," said Andrew. "I'm assuming it's about my dad's lawsuit?"

George shook his head. "Well, sort of. That trial yesterday did not go well, man. He lost, big time. I can only imagine how upset he must have been by that judgment. And then, they decided to stay with the DAO after the trial, so that was kinda the final insult."

"Yeah, that's pretty bad," sighed Andrew. He was about to predict that the next logical step would be to appeal the ruling when George put his hand on Andrew's shoulder. "I hate to tell you, man, but it gets worse. A lot worse. Your father has, uh, well, he has passed away."

"What?! Oh my god. How? And when?"

George was uncharacteristically tongue-tied. "I, er, he...."

"Just tell me," Andrew insisted.

"Well, it looks like he, uh, overdosed on sleeping pills. Just last night."

Andrew frowned and, for a moment, it looked like he might shed tears. He said nothing and slowly shook his head.

After a long pause he exhaled and said quietly, "I *warned* him about those goddamned pills."

George felt especially awkward, given his longtime frustration and resentment over the way that Isaac had cheated him personally. He couldn't bring himself to express a great deal of compassion or sorrow for the passing of a man he had long viewed as an evil bastard.

"It says here he was already dead when his wife found him. And get this: they sent a memo around at work this morning about the importance of mental health care. As if they were implying that it was a suicide."

Oh, *that's* the final insult, right there." Andrew clenched his fist. "Unbelievable."

He sat for a few seconds. The bathroom door opened and Cleo came out and stood next to George, feeling a little awkward. Andrew stood up and straightened his pants. "So," he said, with sudden resolve, "I'm going to head out. Can you help me get that truck returned? I've got the keys here."

George interpreted that to mean 'Can you help me get this machine ready to jump?'

George grabbed his jacket and played along. "Sure. Let's go outside and you show me where the papers are, okay?"

"I'll be back in about 20 minutes. You'll be all right here until then, won't you Cleo?"

"Of course. No worries. Does this record player work?"

"Yeah, knock yourself out." She slid the CSNY album "Déjà vu" out of its jacket and onto the turntable. As the record began to play, she turned to Andrew. I'm really sorry to hear about your dad. I'm sorry for your loss."

"Thank you."

○ ○ ○

The End of Time

One hundred thirty-seven is the inverse of something called the fine-structure constant. ...The most remarkable thing about this remarkable number is that it is dimension-free. ...

Werner Heisenberg once proclaimed that all the quandaries of quantum mechanics would shrivel up when 137 was finally explained.

— LEON M. LEDERMAN

July 2037

George saw the stress in Andrew's expression. "Are you sure you want to leave this morning?"

"I am. Definitely. But, to be honest, I'm really starting to worry that hiding the machine here is a terrible idea. I mean, I must be one of only about 20 people with access to that lab."

"Yeah, but you used that special ID I made for you to gain access to the storage room door, didn't you?"

"Yes. I used it to sign in anonymously at the end of the day, like you suggested."

"Then there's nothing pointing specifically to you."

"Unless there was a camera watching the truck lot or something like that we didn't know about. And besides, I realized that even when I do jump, the you-know-what is going to reappear *here* at some point. And if they watch this place, they're going to see me coming out of this building sooner or later. And then I'm done for."

"Yeah, I can't really argue with that. You could build a tunnel or something, I guess."

"A tunnel?" Andrew frowned at the thought of how much work that would be. "Wouldn't it be better to have it moved to a place where it is not so freaking obvious that it belongs to me?"

"I apologize in advance for this suggestion, but your father could have done it. Does—sorry—*did* he have any property?"

"Quite a bit, actually. Three hundred acres around and including the Andna buildings. But I don't want to besmirch his name just to save my own neck."

Andrew was really getting himself worked up at this point. "Augh, I'm such an idiot. I never should have taken it. They're going to catch me for sure."

"Calm down, bud. Let me think for a moment. What if we moved it to some area of Andna where it might have plausibly been moved, where no one had thought to look? I'm thinking that if it reappears at some point in the future at a location that no one would think was unusual or suspicious, that would solve the whole problem, right?"

"I suppose. Are you suggesting that we smuggle it back *into* the Andna building?"

"I'm still working on that bit. Just a moment, let me think this through."

"The most important thing is that right now, no one knows where it is. And you will be the only one who knows when this thing will reappear. So, as long you get out of here safely right now, you really don't have much to worry about. They can't watch all possible locations all the time forever. So, my advice is: let's get that testing completed and get you out of here ASAP."

"Do you really think so?"

"I do. No sense in putting it off. You can move it again later, when the heat's off."

"All right, let's get those tests underway."

Until Andrew gets his tail in gear and gets safely out of here, George reasoned, there is a risk of this thing being discovered by the police or the FBI and/or whoever else is probably flipping out right now over the possibility of it falling into the hands of a foreign power.

He turned on the power switch and hit a key on his laptop. "Test sequence initiated."

George briefly imagined the seemingly implausible scenario in which powering on the Bubblecraft just now has secretly sent a message to spooks—probably renegade mercenaries or ex-Navy SEALS—hired by the U.S. military, who will then show up in unmarked vans, storm the garage, take them both hostage and throw them and the craft into a large and heavily guarded armored truck on a one-way trip up the ramp and onto a cargo plane ready to take them to Club Fed.

Slam.

Could happen. But even if they *could* track it based on some sort of signature, the fact that Andrew and it will probably both be long gone by the time the Feds get a search warrant and show up here makes the possibility seem like a minimal risk. Best case: not finding it at the expected coordinates would, one would hope, put their entire set of assumptions into question.

Worst case: The Feds arrive while *I'm* still here.

By the time this little scenario played out in his mind, the diagnostic had finished its run and the point was moot.

George set aside his laptop and gave the unit a final visual inspection. "Well, it all checks out. You're good to go whenever you're ready."

"Great. I'll come out with you and make sure the gate is open for you."

o   o   o

The smart meter records confirmed the Bubblecraft's telltale power signature. The computer's display zoomed in on a satellite view of the target location: Andrew's garage. "I have a positive ID on that," the investigator said.

"Send them in," commanded his superior officer.

o   o   o

George retrieved his jacket and laptop as Andrew pulled out the truck keys and handed them to him. "Do you think you can have the truck back before 7 a.m.?" he asked.

"Shouldn't be a problem," said George, as Andrew opened the side door just enough to peer outside. After checking to make sure the coast was clear, they both stepped outside into the crisp night air. Andrew checked that the gate was still open, then walked back to the truck as George opened the driver-side door as quietly as he could. "Where exactly do I return the truck to?"

"It's just a company truck I borrowed," said Andrew. "You don't need to sign for anything or tell anyone. Just park it back in the south-side lot near the other trucks and put the keys back into Erich's drawer. He's away until Tuesday."

"Ha. This is Erich's truck? Nice one." George climbed into the cabin and rolled down the window. He looked at Andrew standing there in the darkness and suddenly felt his fears and his sadness.

"I think it's been more than twenty minutes," said Andrew.

"I guess I should have said thirty or something. No worries. I'll text her. The gate's open, right?"

"Yeah, wide open. I'll lock the gate back up after you're gone."

George shifted rather noisily into reverse and backed the truck out into the lane as Andrew closed and locked the gate.

"Thank you. I'll keep in touch from wherever—whenever—I end up."

Any idea of how far you'll jump?"

"I was thinking a few months. Maybe six or so."

"What about New Year's Eve?"

"Nah, this year has not been a very good one for me. Let's make it next year. We'll do dinner."

George thought for a moment. "Oh, hey, I've got the perfect date: it's literally called The End of Time. It's a 32-bit Unix time-stamp rollover problem sometimes referred to as the Epochalypse[2], and it's happening at exactly 03:14:07 UTC on Tuesday, the 19th of January, 2038. We should do it then."

"Three in the morning?"

"No, that's Universal Time Coordinated, which is equivalent to the old Greenwich Mean Time standard." He did a quick calculation.

"So, that's a five-hour difference from Eastern standard time. So 10:14 p.m. EST on the 18th."

"That's doable, I guess."

"Oh, wait. I have to be in Washington State that week, at a place called Novelty Hill."

"So, you can't make it?"

"No, I could make it... to a place that's in Washington State. I just can't make it to a place near *here*, if this is where you're going to be. Where'll I'll be, it will be 7:14 p.m. Pacific time. I'll be finished work for the day. Just in time for a nice dinner."

[2] 32-bit versions of the Unix timestamp will overflow the largest value that can be held in a signed 32-bit number ($7FFFFFFF^{16}$)

"I could come out there. I'd like to, in fact. Yeah."

"But can you get there?"

"I don't see why not. It's fairly temperate in western Washington at that time of year. Unless there's some sort of epic snowstorm, I think I could be there. Is it a big hill?"

"Well, it's not exactly small, but it's unlikely to be inaccessible."

George reconsidered. "I've got a better place for us to meet, anyway. There's this great little place about ten minutes south of Novelty, in Fall City, right near the highway and easy to get to, with no hills involved. It's called The Last Frontier Roadhouse. Let's meet there. It'll be open for dinner, for sure."

"Well, all right then. 7:14 p.m. PST on Monday, Jan 18 it is."

"A perfect time for dinner and a beer."

"I like it. Till the End of Time then!"

George leaned his arm out of the driver's side window and gave Andrew a thumbs-up sign. "All right. You'd better get going. Good luck."

Andrew stood there for a few seconds with his hands in his jacket pockets.

"Yeah, I've got to get out of here."

"Are you going to leave right now?"

"I think I have to. I'm a nervous wreck worrying about that thing in my garage. The sooner I get out of here with it, the better."

"All right. Get goin'."

"I really should call Rona and see how she's doing before I go. My dad's death must have been a horrible shock to her."

Oh, for god's sake, thought George.

"Yeah, that's rough, man. My sincere condolences. I really should go."

"Thanks again for the help with the diagnostics—and moving this thing."

"I'm just glad you didn't break anything getting it *into* the truck by yourself. That puppy is one expensive ride."

George didn't wait for a response. He rolled up the window and drove away.

o o o

As Andrew walked back from the lane toward the garage, he saw a large black van pull up in front of his house. He watched in alarm as three black-clad figures emerged and began walking toward the front of his house. Cautiously, he made his way to the door on the east side of the garage. His view of the trio of figures was hidden for the moment by the main house between their positions. He unlocked the door as quickly and quietly as he could. Once inside, he locked the door from the inside, jumped into the Bubblecraft cockpit and pulled down the control ring as quickly as he could. As the initialization sequence neared completion, he heard voices and footsteps just outside the door.

Andrew frantically scrolled through the available jump vector values as the agonized sounds of twisting metal and breaking wood pierced the air. A few days would do. He punched the jump control and, just as the door frame began to fall away, there was a blink and suddenly the room was dark and silent again.

Andrew raised the control ring and stepped out of the craft, his heart pounding. He didn't dare to turn on the lights as he inspected the damage to the garage door, which fortunately, didn't interfere with the ability to move the vehicle out via the other door. It seemed too dangerous to go back to his house. Was it even safe to use his cell phone?

He considered boarding up the broken garage door but was too nervous about the noise it would make. Instead, he moved the blue van his father had given him out of the other side of the garage as quickly and quietly as possible, then drove it to George's house.

George could tell at first glance that Andrew was at the end of his wits. "Hey buddy," he said. "What's wrong?"

"The Feds—or the cops—or I dunno, the freakin' men in black—are after me," Andrew sputtered. "I need to move the machine ASAP. Can you help me?"

"Jeez, bud. Calm down. What happened?"

As Andrew attempted to explain the situation, George grew increasingly concerned. "So, you've left the machine unattended in a garage they've already broken into once? Jeez, Andrew! It'll be a miracle if it's still there by the time we get there." George urged him to turn his cell phone off immediately. "For the record," George warned him, "I don't like this and I don't want to *ever* be put in this position again. If they are onto you, they are probably watching our every move, bugging our phones, and who knows what else. They might even be tracking that van you came here in. It's pretty risky for both of us."

Andrew admitted his embarrassment at the situation and apologized.

George shrugged. "Erich's not back until Tuesday. We can use his truck again, I guess. Let's go and get the truck."

o o o

By a stroke of sheer luck, the machine *was* still there when George and Andrew arrived with Erich's truck. It proved a little tricky to move from the side of the garage with the broken door to the other side where the blue van had been, but they managed it. Twenty minutes later, the machine was secured in the back of the truck and on its way to the secure storage locker on the Stern family's property.

"All right," said George. "I'm glad we got that sorted. Never again, agreed?"

Andrew nodded. "See you in January," he said.

At least the new locker was on a piece of private Stern family property and part of a building complex. It wouldn't be so obvious when a person went into the building and didn't come out again. And absolutely no one other than Andrew and George knew about it.

o o o

The blue van pulled up outside of the mailbox office. Andrew got out of the vehicle and entered the building. Inside, he opened a mailbox and retrieved two large envelopes. One had a Land Title and Survey Authority return address, the other was from Wills & Estate Litigation Law, Inc. He riffled through several pieces of junk mail advertising July 4 sales and deposited them in the recycling bin near the door as he left.

He then drove up the pike and took the Princeton Forrestal Center turnoff. About a block away from the main Andna building, he pulled over and stepped out and put on his backpack. He pulled a bicycle out of the back of the van, flipped a makeshift switch near the steering wheel of the van and locked the doors from the outside before pedaling away.

○ ○ ○

That night, Andrew pulled open the storage facility's heavy door just far enough to squeeze inside. Once inside, he turned on his flashlight, pulled the door closed behind him and locked it from the inside. The flashlight's brilliant beam illuminated the titanium alloy tubes of the Bubblecraft frame as he unplugged the charging cable and climbed aboard. He powered it on and tapped on display panel mounted in the control ring to initiate the startup sequence. When the Fibonacci diagram appeared, he selected a displacement factor of 7.65 hours and confirmed the selection. Seconds later, the external power beam lit up the room. The air crackled and, just for a split-second, the dust seemed to come alive as Andrew and the craft disappeared and the room was suddenly dark again.

The next morning at 7:06 a.m., the van's lights suddenly turned on as the ignition light flashed on and P changed to D on the dashboard console. The van silently pulled onto the road and accelerated toward the front window of Andna Corp.

Inside, the security manager and the grounds manager were chatting at the security desk when the van smashed through the window and hurtled toward them. A woman looked up from her cell phone as the van careened toward her. Their coffees spilled as the two managers jumped out of the way as the van's mirror clipped her and knocked her down. As the vehicle crashed into the desk, they rushed over to the woman on the floor.

"This whole area is closed," they heard someone on the other side of the van say as they attended to the woman. "I'm sorry. The whole place is on lockdown. The police are coming..."

"Are you hurt?"

She sat up. "Ouch."

Two days later, at the Novelty Hill facility, an isotope delivery pod disappeared from the accelerator platform. When it reappeared two days later, a bomb hidden inside a packing container went off, destroying the pod and severely damaging the lab.

o o o

POLICE SAY STERN PLANTED BOMB screamed the headline. 'Son's body never found,' said the article. Isaac was believed to have murdered his son and hidden the body somewhere, then killed himself.

The court had found it "inconclusive but probable" that Isaac may also have been responsible for rigging a van registered in his name to drive itself through the building's front window, and for stealing highly confidential materials and U.S. government property.

Andrew closed the newspaper and threw it down on top of the large manila envelopes on the desk. On the side table was a stack of books covering a wide range of philosophies, religions, arts and other disciplines. On top was an open book, showing a few of the many projects of Da Vinci—in particular, his "corkscrew" helicopter design and one of his greatest architectural designs, the magnificent Grand staircase of Chambord.

On each of the facing pages were similar illustrations of a helix and a yin-yang–like symbol. The design of both the corkscrew and the staircase resembled a yin-yang symbol— and, from the side, the staircase was a double helix.

It was time to get going again.

o o o

The lawyer slid a stack of papers across the table toward Andrew. "Thank you for getting in touch, Mr. Stern," he said. "We were, of course, concerned when we heard the rumors that you were missing and presumed dead. There are no charges or liens outstanding against Andrew Stern and you, your mother, and Isaac's widow were listed as beneficiaries in the Will, which we have found to be in good order. However, as you may know, your father appears to have authored a suicide note, found some time after his death, showing that he was solely responsible for the theft and subsequent sale of a device identified as 'Bubblecraft' and the terrorist activities at the Princeton and Redmond facilities. Are these actions that you think he would have been capable of taking?"

"I suppose so."

The lawyer went through the papers with Andrew, indicating where he needed to sign or initial.

"All right. The prenup agreements with Mrs. Caroline Stern—that's your birth mother, right? —and Mrs. Rona Wells Stern were both found to be valid and uncontested and neither party has contested the portion of the funds and lands lawfully assigned to you under the terms of his Last Will and Testament."

"Yes, she said she always knew I was alive."

"Well, good for her. All right. Your money should be in your bank account in the next week or two. You'll have to call the police and give them this affidavit, explaining why you couldn't be found."

"Vacation."

"I guess we're done. The lawyer closed his notepad and stood up. "How is your mom, anyway?"

"She's sad that he took his life. She said she misses him."

"Yeah, it's rough. And you're making out okay?"

"Yes, thanks. Bye now."

"We'll take care of the paperwork to get the estate closed out and the deeds signed over to you. Thanks for coming in."

Twelve days later, Andrew found 954.1 million dollars in his personal bank account.

o o o

9

Skyscraper Shadows

September 2037

George had done unusual things before, but never anything like this.

Rumors circulated at the company that he had been fired after being caught attempting to leave the premises with an unauthorized backup. Others had heard that this was just a cover story—that he'd been moved into a top-secret project. When the company confirmed that he had left, no one would say where or why he had gone. Some accused management of yet another publicity stunt; others tracked him to Houston, where they said the trail went dark.

It went dark only because that was the way George wanted it to be. In fact, he had moved to a suburb on the south side of Houston called Skyscraper Shadows, just a few blocks from the William P. Hobby Airport and had taken a position working on top-secret projects at the Space Center eleven miles southeast of there. One of the projects was to lead a team in adapting the Bubblecraft tech for use in deep space, the other was to help NASA engineers get their quantum communication system—now dubbed Qmunications—working.

NASA firmly believed—as George did, too—that deep space travel was the killer app for 'fast forward' temporal travel. Being able to put an astronaut, or an entire colony, for that matter, on a long-distance journey to a distant star or planet and have them arrive within a human lifespan was finally within the realm of the possible. It was like hibernation without all the health and wellness problems that entailed. The applications for temporal travel in space were almost limitless.

The ever-optimistic theorists speculated that the current iteration's "forward-only" limitation would, in time, be worked around. Indeed, many of NASA's most ambitious plans depended upon it. They imagined fast-grown off-world food plantations, fast-decaying radioactive waste disposal facilities, fast-manufacturing facilities in space, fast interplanetary delivery services and more.

Even among those who restricted themselves only to what was currently possible saw flash-forward tech as rich in potential. The pitch decks presented by those who were privy to the existence of the one-way temporal tech were overflowing with ultra-long-term plans to create new Utopias wherever humans dared to venture.

They implored the executives to imagine the possibilities if a trip around the solar system took as little time as a bus trip to the park; if planetary-scale terraforming projects didn't take 10,000 years, but instead were ready to inhabit in a day or two. Terraforming a nearby planet or moon wouldn't seem nearly as hard when the end result was so close. Interplanetary travel would become less of a logistical problem and more of a physics and chemistry challenge.

And as the PowerPoint presentations and feasibility studies came and went, the approval for a new aeronautics and space-time research administration was granted and ASTRA was born.

The new NASA division had a mission statement as bold as that of John F. Kennedy's in the 1960s: to land an American on a planet in another solar system by the end of the century.

o o o

"The basic idea of the project," explained George to the Qmunications project team, "is to entangle a pair of electrons and then send one of them forward in time, then use the principle of quantum teleportation to work around the issues leading to the so-called quantum no-communication theorem."

"The device that actually makes the connection to initiate the communication link," he explained, "is a low-energy electron gun with an entangling module and a transmitter/receiver contained in a small box that will eventually be built into larger shipping containers and various types of vehicles."

He displayed a project timeline on the screen behind him. "For the first round of tests, the device will automatically send an arbitrary message. For the second series of tests, we will enable the onboard sensors and collect actual status reports in a variety of conditions, both ideal and adverse. The final round of tests," he explained, "will include transmission and validation of both manually entered status reports and automatic sensor readings." He estimated that this phase would begin soon after the seventh successful test.

○ ○ ○

George looked up from his notebook to see Andrew arguing with a woman at the counter. "No, I pay good money for first-class tickets precisely so I do *not* have to arrange the seating, eating, and baggage details for the trip myself. And I do *not* want to use the automated system to register my passport and an additional piece of picture ID. I'm not even leaving the country."

George approached the counter. "Hey, don't mind my associate. It's been a very long day. Is there someone we could ask for help, please?"

Andrew glared at George, but backed off. He'd seen enough evidence of George's persuasive ways with women.

"Yes sir, I'll be able to help you right after I check these people in," said the woman.

"That sound fine, thanks. Miss... Jemma. You're doing a great job."

She smiled. "Ticket, please?"

○ ○ ○

On the flight, George told Andrew about the Qmunications project he had been working on. "Man, you're gonna love this code: the system lets you perform asynchronous communication as a cross-temporal link."

Andrew seemed skeptical. "What about the no-communication theorem?"

"Oh, you know about that? Top points for you, my man." George grinned. "Thing is, I'm not using that method. I'm doing what is technically known as quantum teleportation, but with a zero distance. And it works. After jumping forward in time, you can still communicate with the jump-point in the past."

"Really?"

"Just think of what we can do with that, man," George whispered excitedly. "We can send ourselves the winning lottery numbers—or *any* kind of information. Nothing physical, though—just information."

"Just be careful. I don't want to see you end up in jail."

"Nah, you can't charge a person for a crime they haven't committed yet."

"It going to seem awfully suspicious if they find out about the time travel stuff."

"They won't—it's top secret," George fibbed. "Besides, I've got an idea. What if we sent messages that weren't obviously suspicious looking? You know, encode a lottery number as the letter-count in the words in a sentence or something like that."

"I don't follow. What?"

"I mean something like this: Let's say we are going to

send the number 2875. We could encode it in the number of characters—ignoring punctuation—in each word. Like this: 'An imbecile couldn't count.' Or, if we wanted to send text —and perhaps make it a little trickier to decode—we could use an offset value. 'Hoping perpetually, I am as a number. Fortunately, I am in 3.' The last number on the line is the offset value, so add that value to the letter-count of each of the words to get the letter count of the decoded word. For example, a one-character word is A+(offset), so A+(3) = D. And so on."

"That's brilliant, buddy. Perfect. You be in charge of writing the sentences, and I'll get the code working."

o · o · o

George warned that it was 'a hack,' but 48 hours later, he had a working version of the cross-temporal communications code. He briefed Andrew on how to send a message and set the jump meridian for two days. They booked time at the Princeton facility's newly repaired temporal test lab and George watched as his friend disappeared from the transit pad. The post-transit status light flashed, indicating a quantum qubit had been sent by the transit pod, now two days in the future, and observed at the starting-point station. Then, three more flashes. The decoder ran and seconds later, a message appeared on the screen:

PING

George typed his reply and hit send. Two days in the future, the message appeared on Andrew's screen:

PONG

Two days later, they raised their glasses. "To our very first successful test!"

An hour later, NASA researchers were elated when a message from George arrived on their receiving terminal.

"This message was sent from five minutes in the future."

In addition to sending messages only to the quantum backchannel receiver, George also wrote a subroutine that forwarded each message as an anonymous post on the Pastebin site.

"Brilliant!" enthused Andrew. It was the breakthrough they'd all been waiting for.

"Man, this is too good. I don't want to jump forward until we show this to the folks at ASTRA. They're going to love it."

George very generously included Andrew's name in the credits for the code and this led to an increasing number of invitations and commendations from the engineers and program managers at Andna, ASTRA, and even Cornerstone.

In December 2037, Andrew was offered a position on the Andna board of directors. Suddenly, he, too, didn't want to jump forward any great lengths of time. Microjumping did help him with his jetlag, though.

o o o

Imagine an intergalactic communications system, capable of near-instantaneous data transmission across virtually unlimited distances with no signal loss. That's what space-faring startup ASTRA, in conjunction with New Jersey-based Andna Corporation claim to have developed. In announcing the breakthrough quantum teleportation technology at a NASA-funded press conference, Qmunications codeveloper Andrew Stern claimed the new tech was just the beginning of the company's efforts to revolutionize interplanetary communications. Beam us up!

○ ○ ○

Did you know?

The Andna board of directors reportedly didn't want to reveal the complete set of Qmunications capabilities that a full disclosure would have required.

○ ○ ○

Happy New Year! George wrote. *Don't forget our dinner Jan 18 at the Last Frontier.*
I'll be there, Andrew replied, *before the end of time.*

○ ○ ○

10

Fall City

January 2038

About fourteen minutes southeast of the big data centers of Redmond Ridge lies the town of Fall City. George and Andrew were there, sitting at the bar at the Last Frontier Roadhouse on Monday, 18 January 2038 when all hell broke loose.

At 7:14:07 p.m. Pacific Standard Time, a Pi symbol appeared on all the TVs for eight seconds. Then the power went off.

A woman at the end of the bar broke the sudden silence. "Hey, I think you blew a fuse."

The bartender came out from behind the bar and peered out the front window. "I don't think so. The lights are off next door, too."

As he raised the blinds to let in more light, he looked out the window at the gas station, where a would-be gas-pumper stood in the shadows.

George tried to check the news on his phone. "This is weird. No service."

He showed it to Andrew. "Jesus. Must be a big outage."

The sound of air brakes startled Andrew as a freight truck rolled noisily to a stop outside. A moment later a trucker opened the door of the saloon and stepped into the dark room. "Damn. This ain't good."

"Howdy," said the bartender, wiping the counter.

"Still pourin' beers?"

The bartender picked up a glass. "What'll it be?"

"Just a draft."

"Pint?"

"Sounds good."

The bartender filled the glass and set it down in front of the trucker. "Any idea what's going on out there?"

"On channel 9 on the CB, they think it may be a terrorist thing."

"Were those Pi symbols on the TVs here, too?"

"Yeah, just for a few seconds."

"Yep, eight seconds, I hear. They're callin' it the eight-second war. Apparently, that happened all over the country—and Canada, too. I jus' wanted to see it for myself. So, your phones are dead, too?" They nodded. "Damn."

o o o

The trucker finished his beer and checked his phone. Still dead.

He pulled a five-dollar bill from his pocket and dropped it on the counter. "Welp, gotta go. Hope your lights come on soon."

The barman turned a key on his cash register and the cash drawer opened. "Well, that's a relief."

George leaned in to take a closer look at the register. "Those things have a backup battery, don't they?"

"Yeah, but it's just for the totals and merchant code—stuff like that. I guess we're cash only for a while."

Andrew slid a $20 bill across the bar. "Keep the change."

"Come on," he said to George. "Let's get back to the Inn and find out what the hell's going on."

As they stepped outside, traffic was heavy along Fall City Road. At the gas and electric station, several large trucks had pulled up in front of the pumps and charging stands. The drivers stood in a semicircle, talking.

As George and Andrew approached, one of the truckers nodded his head in acknowledgement of their presence. The others turned as George spoke. "Hey, any news about what's goin' on?"

"Not much," said the trucker who noticed them first. "There's some talk that this might be a date rollover bug or something that knocked the power grid offline. Like a computer bug kinda thing. 'The Y2038 problem' I've heard it called."

"That seems pretty hard to believe," scoffed one of the other truckers.

George knew about the Unix time issue and he found it impossible to believe that this could be blamed solely on that. "Yeah, I agree," said George. "It's damned strange, but given that Pi symbol on the TVs, I think it's safe to say that it was an intentional attack. It was, after all, pi time."

"What do you mean, 'pie time?'" asked one of the truckers.

"If the exact time of the outage is specified in Coordinated Universal Time—known as UTC—then this outage occurred at exactly 3:14:15 UTC. 3.1415... get it? That's "Pi time." It is highly unlikely that this could be a coincidence. It would be kind of amusing if it weren't obviously a *fucking terrorist act.*"

"UTC? That's like Greenwich Mean Time, ain't it?"

"Kind of. UTC is a time standard; GMT is a time zone, but yeah, the offset is the same."

"Your CB radios are still working, aren't they?" asked Andrew.

"Yeah, but not every truck has one these days. Most of us do, though."

"Well, good luck."

When they crossed the street to the Roadhouse Inn, it too was dark. Inside, the assistant manager stood near the desk. A few candles burned around the counter area and she held a flashlight. George dangled his key on his finger as he passed her. "We've got a couple of rooms upstairs. Have you got an extra flashlight?"

She shook her head. "I'll take you there," she offered.

"We do have a generator," she said as they climbed the stairs. "We're just setting it up now." She opened the fire door leading to the second-floor hallway. "Won't be long. The elevators will be out of service, though."

By the time they reached their rooms, they could hear the sound of the generator starting up. A few of the lights flickered back on. "We've turned a few of the non-essential lights off, y'see? It's just to save power. If possible, please don't use the coffeemaker or any unnecessary electrical appliances. We'll have a pot o' coffee down in the lobby for y'all, okay?"

"Great, thanks," said George as he turned the key and opened the door to his room. "Come on in," he said to Andrew.

Inside, George grabbed the radio and turned it on. He turned the dial back and forth looking for radio stations. Nothing. He picked up the phone on the desk and inspected the connection on the back. He lifted the receiver to his ear and pressed the hang-up button a few times. "This is a regular old land-line phone. This should be working."

Suddenly, a discordant pair of tones shattered the silence. "Holy shit, that's my cell phone."

"Yeah, mine too."

"Took them long enough."

George tried tuning the radio again. It, too, was now broadcasting the Emergency Alert System attention signal tones.

"That is the most annoying sound."

"This is the Emergency Broadcast System. Please stay tuned for further information as it becomes available."

A text message appeared on Andrew's phone. "Local authorities are working to address widespread power and service outages. Please be patient." A few seconds later, a vaguely robotic voice repeated the same information on the radio, first in English, then Spanish, and then a language they didn't recognize. "Is that Chinese?"

"I'm not sure. But I do know that Chinese is number three by percentage of the population. It's definitely unusual. These things are usually in English only."

"This would be a perfect future-news report to send to your followers," said George.

"For sure! Oh, I wish I could send that message right now."

George was thinking practically. "Maybe if there's power back at the new lab on Novelty Hill, the transit pod might still be linked." He scratched his head. "I dunno. Maybe."

"It's like 15 minutes away. It's worth a try."

o o o

When they arrived at the Novelty Hill lab, the parking lot was almost empty. A pair of security guards checked their ID at the front door and cautioned them that many services were unavailable. Fortunately, the data center at Novelty Hill was virtually identical to the one in Princeton, including the failsafe system for the lab and server farm, which was now running on generator power. Andrew checked again for cell-phone or internet service, to no avail. Here, too, some sort of catastrophic collapse of the power grid and communications systems had obviously occurred. There was still precious little information available, although an emergency warning system status update on their phones now characterized the power outages as 'national.'

George logged in as 'Name not available' and checked the

Qmunications management console. "It's still running, and the entangled bits and the classical communications channels are both still undisturbed. Uptime is fourteen days, three hours and twenty-one minutes."

"Great," said Andrew, typing on the console keyboard. "So, this might actually work."

"Yep. Let me know when you're ready to transmit."

"Power is nominal, systems are online and good to go."

Andrew finished typing the message, ominously titled *The Omega Event: Power in Peril*. In it, he named the exact start and end time and date of what was now being called the 8-second war. And in an attempt to be poetic, he described Pi as symbolic of 'the circle of depravity at the heart of this war on decency.'

He couldn't decide how to attribute the prophetic missive; in the end he went with the only pseudonym he could come up with that slyly referenced his time-traveling credentials: he signed off as *Won Yong Han*.

"Okay," he announced. "Ready to send."

"Here goes."

o o o

11

The 8-second War

> The physical Universe does seem to be organised around elegant mathematical relationships. And one number above all others has exercised an enduring fascination for physicists: 137.0359991…. It is known as the fine-structure constant and is denoted by the Greek letter alpha (α)
>
> — PAUL DAVIES

January 2038

When the warning about the "Omega Event" was received two weeks earlier, it was initially dismissed as just another paranoid conspiracy theory. But when the startling predictions came true, the text of this message traveled by word of mouth far and wide. It was the message that cemented Won Yong Han as a *bona fide* prophet, despite the irony of the internet being offline almost everywhere in the world the day the prophecy came true.

Indeed, the near-complete collapse of the internet was something that most people had believed impossible. But, as media and communications services slowly came back online and reports emerged from various sources, people began to put together a picture of what, it seemed, had happened.

It appeared that the attackers had used a globally distributed approach. IP addresses were traced to proxies in the Middle East, North Korea, China, Russia, and elsewhere, including one linked to a Hezbollah group based in Moscow. Due to the complexity of the various malware agents used, researchers were uncertain of the attack's origin point, but the Moscow connection loomed as a likely contender.

The motivation was unclear—at least at first. It was widely speculated that only a superpower nation-state could mount such a sophisticated offensive. The attack bore strong similarities to earlier malware attacks on critical infrastructures that had been linked to a Russian government-backed research institute. Some contended that hackers affiliated with the group *Anonymous* were to blame.

The incriminating evidence was a blog entry posted two days earlier by someone claiming to be a member of the group, expressing 'public safety concerns' over the emergence of truly sentient artificial intelligence connected to the power grid and national infrastructure.

The allegations gained credibility a day later when another *Anonymous*-affiliated blog responded to the rumors. The attack, it claimed, was a protest by radicalized ultraconservatives against the recent 'transhumanist' trends in genetic modification and cerebral augmentation.

Everyone with an agenda was suddenly suspect. And then there were those who cared little for the politics and even less for the science. To the average person, the days following the simultaneous failure of the power grids in most of the major urban centers around the world and the communications networks seemed at first to be little more than an inconvenience. But each day thereafter, reports about newly discovered data losses and widespread database corruptions became more and more common. The malware was pernicious and incredibly sophisticated. It had infected virtually every database and website exposed to the internet.

The hacks that followed at these infection points—by whoever had executed them—had been astoundingly deep and far-reaching. A huge amount of information—including virtually all internet protocol traffic—was corrupted in such a way that anti-virus tools saw it as malicious and attempted to block it entirely. The top-level internet domains were completely compromised, the names on all the major domain name services wiped out. The stock market collapsed; the banking system fell in pandemonium.

Around the globe, transportation companies and businesses of every type were suddenly cast into disarray as an estimated 95 percent of internet services were unavailable. And internet-sweeping worms hosted on vast botnets of compromised desktop computers took out a few more percent in the hours and days that followed, as backups were compromised as soon as they came online. George marveled at the brilliance and sheer scope of the hack. This *had* to be state sponsored.

Seventeen hours after the attack hit, the private-line phone at the Andna office in Princeton rang. "Put me through to Erich Rössler. Tell him it's Bob from Cornerstone. It's urgent. Thank you."

"Hello Bob. This is Erich."

"Erich, I'm glad you've still got power to your phones there. This power outage has really played hell with our systems here. That's why I'm calling, in fact. Who's in charge of the AI division there, these days?"

"Uh, well, as you may have heard, the company recently reorganized as a decentralized autonomous organization. Unfortunately, that system is currently offline, so, the local members of our former board of directors are managing the situation at the moment. As the company doesn't have a president or VP, the various divisions, such as the ones under my purview, are currently being managed directly by the directors. So, I'll do my best to help you. What do you need?"

"Well, that AI you folks licensed to us is having some issues that have us baffled, and we're wondering if we can talk to someone on the XAVR team there. I need to speak to whoever's in charge of our military contract."

Erich realized this was not a good time to tell Bob that he had recently fired George.

"Bob, I'm going to put you through directly to the head programmer for military ops, George Gunderson."

"That sounds good. Is he there?"

"I'll see if he is available. Please hold."

○ ○ ○

George was standing in the control room of the rebuilt temporal lab at Novelty Hill when the land-line phone rang. He looked at the caller ID on the display. Ha! Erich was calling. Typical. He decided not to take his call. Maybe Erich would think twice before firing him next time.

o o o

Erich couldn't get through to George. He pressed the Quick Dial number for the lab downstairs. No answer. He looked at his phone's clock. It was just after 9:30 a.m. Eastern Time. He tried calling Li Yan Zhang, then Karl Schraeder. No connection in both cases. Erich sighed and punched the button for line 1. "Sorry for the delay, Bob. The cell phone network in his area seems to be down. I'll get him or someone else who can help you to call back as soon as possible. Can we reach you at this number?"

"Yes. We can get him online via the secure network, which will be required anyway. I'll send you the access codes, in case he contacts you first."

o o o

Twenty-two minutes later, George and Andrew called Erich from the secure line at the Novelty Hill server room. "Hey Erich. I finally found a working phone," George fibbed. "Have you been trying to reach me?"

"Yes, thanks for checking in."

"Of course."

"Look," said Erich, "we've got to get back to Bob from

Cornerstone. Can you call him and then let me know what he needs, exactly? I'll be here."

George looked at the clock. It was just after 12:40 p.m. Pacific time.

"Bob. This is George Gunderson. Erich asked me to call you ASAP. How can I help you?"

"We've got a non-functioning AI executive here. Is that something you can take a look at?"

"Have you rebooted the system?"

"No, we haven't done anything yet. It auto-disconnected as soon as the attack was detected."

"That's good. That's what it is supposed to do. I'll take a look."

"Can you do that right away? We're in a pickle here."

"Yes, I will. I'll call you at your number there in half an hour or so. Goodbye."

George set up a system completely isolated from the corporate network and logged into the military system. As soon as he connected, the malware began scanning his network connection for open ports. George's system was set up with multiple virtualized operating system environments—each running in an isolated sandbox and connected via a dedicated network card. Amazingly, the malware almost immediately compromised the integrity of his test system, as it wormed its way into vulnerable subsystems and services.

"Wow, that shouldn't be possible. Look at this, Andrew. That was supposedly a fully patched BSD virtual machine running on a Secure BSD host. It compromised both the sandbox OS *and* the host. Very impressive. And look at the network packets coming in—eighty-seven million requests per second."

"Yeah, that's fairly impressive. Is that a record?"

"Maybe. There have been bigger swarm attacks, but not sustained like this—at least the ones that have been reported."

"Is the military system infected?"

"I can't tell. Probably."

When George called Bob back, all he could say was that their system appeared to be compromised and that they should wipe everything and restore from a backup.

o o o

In the days that followed, the phone systems, radio and TV services came back online and stories of bravery and suffering during the widespread blackouts dominated the news. George managed to make headway in his investigation, but Bob hit the roof while George was giving his third daily status report.

"Sick of the weasel words" was how Bob put it. Andna, he insisted, was negligent, if not complicit. Lawsuits were threatened, then filed, demanding compensation for breaches of essential services.

Unfortunately, one of the essential services interrupted was George's email. Incoming new messages were suddenly corrupted and vanished. He was able to recover a few incomplete portions of some of the messages. One was from an anonymized remailer. Beyond that, George couldn't tell who it was from. But its message intrigued him. "I am alive," it said.

Meanwhile, in the news, the parties on the radical right were now blaming artificially evolved humans. After speculation arose that an attack of this level of sophistication must have been the work of either AI or cerebrally enhanced humans, they called to have both machine intelligence and cerebral augmentation banned entirely. Religious fringe groups called it the apocalypse. And, after details emerged of exactly where and how the attack spread, the U.S. government put a moratorium on all AI-based connections to the power grid and defense systems, so fearful had the populace become of the automation in which they were so heavily invested.

A surprising result of the actions taken following these events was a significant upswing in "no-tech" activism. They rallied against the perceived evils of automation, citing jobs lost and rights abused. They championed privacy concerns. The extremists blamed pretty much everything on the internet.

While George was holed up in the Novelty Hill office working on the Cornerstone situation, Andrew kept himself busy by writing new prophecies about major events as they unfolded. He enjoyed the furor that his missives created. As it became increasingly indefensible to label him as a crackpot, conspiracy theories about him began to hit the mainstream media. *He* was the hacker, thought some. Others called him the chosen one. Andrew liked the sound of that.

o o o

Many internet-based services and data repositories remained offline, and banking and financial services were slow to return to regular hours of service, but by the beginning of August, the world slowly returned to a sense of near-normalcy. Even the notoriously problem-plagued airline system computers were back online.

When the airplanes started flying again, Andrew told George he was planning to head home to New Jersey. By this point, George had done just about everything he could do to get Cornerstone's systems up and running again. The AI executive was hobbled by the government's new restrictions, but *c'est la vie*.

∘ ∘ ∘

George stayed in contact with Andrew, and Andrew paid him well in return for technical support.

One Friday afternoon in August, a message arrived. "Hey buddy," it said. "I have to do some work on the new temporal lab at the NASA Space Center for a few days. Do you want to come down there with me and take a look at it? I know a couple of girls that work there. Could be fun."

"That sounds good," Andrew wrote back. "Do you think we should fly down there this weekend?"

"Yeah, for sure. Can you book us a flight for tomorrow?"

Andrew's digital assistant answered: "I can get a couple of first-class tickets on American Airlines, 8:45 a.m. tomorrow."

"Great. We'll have to rent a car when we get there, too. I haven't got any wheels in Houston right now. I'll get you a guest pass to the lab."

When they arrived, Andrew rented a car, turned off the self-driving features, and drove while George sat in the passenger seat and wrote a set of scripts that added one or more names to the temporal lab guest list.

"Why did you turn that off?" George asked.

"I'm just not...." Andrew said, his words trailing off into muted anxiety. George had been that expression before. didn't pursue the topic and Andrew said nothing more until they arrived at George's new digs on the south side of Houston known as Skyscraper Shadows.

o o o

After a few days with George and his girlfriends, Andrew was ready to return home.

"I'm going to head back tomorrow, I think," he told George.

"Hey man," said his friend, "I'm really glad you came down. That was a blast."

George leaned close and whispered. "You've still got that *thing* in storage, yeah?"

Andrew nodded.

He explained to George that he was anxious to find a more secure location for the Bubblecraft. It needed a permanent home.

In truth, he'd been feeling increasingly nervous about keeping the Bubblecraft on private property traceable to him. That had to change.

He told George he'd decided to move it to the secure storage facility on his grandfather's property near the Andna buildings. That way, he reasoned, if it was ever discovered, he could plausibly argue that it must have been moved there without his knowledge or permission. Nobody else needed to know that he had the only key.

"Sounds like a plan," said George. "I'll be there next week. Let's move it on the weekend, when it's quiet around there."

o o o

12

The Prophecies

2038

A few hours later, George's phone pinged. It was a response from Cleo. She was seeing someone else.

Andrew's phone rang. "Hey, George. What's up?"

"That's it, I'm done," said George.

"Did you solve their problem?"

"God, no. Erich fired me again."

"What?! You can't be serious."

"Well, that Bob guy was pissing me off. I got a bit snippy with him."

"Oh my god. What are you gonna *do*?"

"Well, what do you say we fire that puppy of yours up and get the hell out of here?"

"Really, you want to?"

"Definitely."

"Yeah, screw them. You don't need them."

"Well, let's just go then. We'll just head up there to your place and we can do the jump together."

"I haven't bought my plane ticket yet. Do you want to fly up?"

"Yeah, for sure. You don't wanna drive from here to Princeton with me in a car. We'd be at each other's throats by the time we got there, believe me. Especially at this time of the year."

o   o   o

Andrew felt far less paranoid of having the machine stolen or discovered now that George had figured out how to disable the onboard GPS that he believed was the reason the feds had been able to track the device when it was in his old garage. Now that it was properly secured, he began using it to microjump forward more frequently, usually just a few hours or days at a time. That was enough to be first to buy or sell a stock, or have a story ready on a breaking news topic before anyone else. Short delays weren't as embarrassing to explain when someone was expected a timely response, either.

At this point, the audience for Won Yong Han's missives was comprised strictly of ASTRA devs and Andna engineers that had the required top-secret security clearance. At first, this was a very small group, all of which had been instructed on how to minimize any possibility of creating paradox events. The group was instructed not to be specific in terms of any personally identifiable information or event details.

Still, however, the stories he sent back using George's Qmunications system did make *some* impact—small at first, but it didn't take long for outside bloggers to begin posting their own hot takes on the latest 'prophecies' via social media. And once the prophecies started coming true, they took on a life of their own. They were vague, but they weren't *that* vague. It became obvious to his followers that these prophecies were the real deal.

Sure, the NASA staff who leaked the temporal transmissions were violating their non-disclosure agreements that very clearly stipulated that they were strictly forbidden from mentioning the existence of the top-secret back-messaging technology, but as the inevitable leaks spread, a growing body of people started believing that these messages were genuine prophecies.

The media, fed by leaked reports from anonymous sources and disgruntled employees, dubbed the pseudonymous author 'The New Nostradamus' and the mysterious prophet's online fanbase soon grew into a cult.

○ ○ ○

George may have been fired from Erich's team in Princeton, but his programming skills were still in demand across Andna and its partner organizations. He regularly accepted contracts in Redmond and Houston and often found himself on a panel with his old HELX teammates or his friend and new board member Andrew. For one such panel, Andrew and George were both flown first class to Redmond, where they were invited to sit in on some of the meetings with committees and groups that Andrew's father had been instrumental in organizing.

One of the most obvious themes apparent in many of these meetings was the importance that Isaac Stern had placed upon temporal travel planning and risk mitigation.

There was, of course, a significant risk that a wall, a radioactive cloud, or even an ocean or mountain would appear at the target destination, or that no one would be there to assist in case of an intersection event (now the preferred term for the type of event formerly known as an accident). There was, unfortunately, no way to know. However, it was generally agreed by those on the risk mitigation committee that the least distant destination vector should be equipped with both automatic and manual "forwarding" options, just in case. In other words, if an intersection event was detected at the destination vector, the program would auto-route forward to the next available jump-vector, *ad infinitum* (or, in the case of the Bubblecraft, as long as power was available). It wasn't ideal, but it was better than intersecting with a pile of rubble.

Another strong theme in the late Dr. Stern's planning efforts was evangelization of the technology's potential benefits. It had seemed so logical, so important to Isaac Stern that scientists and social planners alike would prepare and be ready for widespread commercial adoption of this breakthrough technology. How could they do otherwise?

As Andrew reviewed his father's notes he found a meticulously kept list of those with whom Isaac or Erich Rössler had shared the details about the temporal tech. Even within the company, the list of people who knew about the temporal transit project was very limited.

He had evangelized the project ceaselessly to anyone with

top-secret clearance, but even in those cases, he had required attendees and demonstrators alike to sign a non-disclosure agreement. Still, the university's business manager hired three lobbyists and a space scientist named Dr. Marjorie Blint to work on finding potential candidates for future disclosure within the government and both North American and European academic channels. The lobbyists joined the scientists and engineers on the project that teleconferenced into the meeting that George and Andrew attended, where each participant reported on the latest "flash forward" trends and applications. And, of course, the development of a working Qmunications system was big news. Dr. Blint seemed particularly impressed to see Andrew Stern credited as a co-author.

Five months later, the governance committee comprised of representatives from Andna LLC, in cooperation with the European Organisation for Nuclear Research announced what they called the world's longest-term international non-military fundamental research project, dubbed EON Research.

The European media dubbed EON Research as one of the top 10 companies to watch. A few months later, there was an opportunity to work on another top-secret project for the managers of the ASTRA division at NASA.

After the success of the Qmunications project, NASA was eager to hire George as a contractor again to work on a related issue: teleportation. After all, they were essentially already doing quantum teleportation, but with a distance factor of zero. The measure of success in this project, the project lead explained, is to get that number to anything *other* than zero.

To George, it seemed that the problem was primarily a logistical one. Given that the experimental results must be observed entirely *in situ*, he reasoned that performing a time-jump with an already moving vehicle might be the easiest solution. That way, a precisely interpolated time and position could be derived anywhere between the start and end times and points. He developed an algorithm he called 'time tweening' to calculate intermediate positions along the time-scale. As a proof-of-concept, he whipped up a simple animation showing how a time jump could affect a moving spacecraft.

Fortunately, this type of experimental result was exactly what NASA was aiming for. They gave the go-ahead on the project and moved George onto the space-based research team.

The first tests used a transit pod on a movable dolly. Disappointingly, the results appeared at the exact spatial coordinates of the original transmission, but at a different time. In other words, as soon as the receiver was moved, it stopped working. But results were more encouraging when the receiver remained stationary and the transmitting device was moved. In this case, the time-space position of the transmitter and receptor, the period and duration of transmission, and the proper functioning of both transmitting and receiving equipment all proved to be critical factors that led to the first successful test.

As Earth, and indeed, the entire solar system, are whirling through the galaxy, these problems were not trivial in nature. But, short-term "forwarding" of data streams, to receptors just nanoseconds away, proved the viability of the technology and the underlying principle.

The next step was the construct long-distance data transmission opportunities. As it turned out, the rotation of the earth proved a useful way to generate previously unachievable jump-periods and progress was rapid in these heady early days. Moving to the use of space-based transmission equipment yielded another leap in time projection, but claimed the life of Dr. Emil Fidor, Stern's counterpart at CERN, who was reportedly killed in a space-station depressurization accident during one such test.

○ ○ ○

2040

During the months leading up to the Qmunications announcement, Andrew and Marjorie had been seeing a lot of each other at board meetings and, later, in more intimate settings.

Marjorie was highly supportive of Andrew's efforts to earn a doctoral degree. She knew firsthand how much work goes into a doctorate in physics. When he finally obtained his PhD, he and Dr. Blint celebrated by sending a bottle of champagne through the machine, and giving the facility staff the rest of the day off.

The following June, Andrew and Marjorie decided to make it official and got married in Carmel, California. After the cutting of the cake and the obligatory speeches, thank-yous and toasts, Marjorie congratulated Andrew publicly on his PhD.

Everyone toasted Dr. Stern. The DJ spun their special song—the David Archuleta rendition of *Love Me Tender*—and they stepped out onto the dance floor.

Later that night, George and his date whirled past them on the dancefloor. After the dance, George introduced the shapely brunette. "This is Carla from Redmond." She reminded Andrew a little of George's old girlfriend Cleo. "You look gorgeous," she said to Marjorie.

Andrew and Marjorie left the reception after another hour or so of dancing; George and Carla had already left. Andrew and Marjorie ran into them in the hotel restaurant the next morning. "How long are you two here?" Carla asked.

"We'll be around Carmel for another week. What about you?"

"I've got a flight to catch in about two and a half hours. Congratulations, you guys." Carla hugged George. "I'll send you a picture when I get home," she whispered in his ear.

Near the front door of the hotel, the valet pulled up in a convertible—a rental, by the look of it—and Carla pressed a bill into his hand as he stood near the open driver's side door. She threw her bag into the passenger seat and waved at them as the valet closed the door for her. She put on her sunglasses and pulled the car out of the *porte-cochere*.

"I'll see you guys later," George said to Andrew and Marjorie. "I'm heading to my room, and then I'm heading up to Silicon Valley. I might stop in Monterey, too. I'll see you before the end of the week. Awesome wedding, by the way."

"Hey, I was thinking," said Marjorie, "we should make a pact to all get together again at some point in the future."

"That's an awesome idea. How far in the future?"

"Why don't we shoot for the end of 2999?" suggested Andrew.

"December 31, 2999? That's so sentimental of you. How cute is that?" teased Marjorie. "You know that's not actually the beginning of the new millennium, right?"

"I know. But still—the end of the thirtieth century! And then the millennium will follow the year after that. I don't want to miss that, either."

"All in good time," George said, realizing he sounded like Kaedra.

"I love it," she said. "So, we're all agreed—New Year's Eve, 2999?"

"Sounds good to me. Where do you want to meet?"

"Somewhere warm!" suggested Marjorie.

"I'd imagine the Houston Space-Time Center will still be there," said George. "We all know where that is and it should at least be above freezing. Let's meet in front of the main building—or if it's not there, where it *used* to be—at, say, noon, Houston time."

"Perfect. See you then!"

"Bye George."

"Good luck, you two."

"Thanks again, buddy."

In their hotel room later that evening, Marjorie stripped off her wedding gown. "We should be the first people in the world to time-travel while having sex. We could set a world record."

"Oh, you want a world record?" he winked.

"No pressure," she laughed.

"And then Guinness will tell everybody?"

"Not everybody. Strictly adults only."

"So, we're adults all of a sudden?"

She looked at the new ring on her finger. "Yeah, I guess so. Hey, when do you think we should jump?"

"We can go whenever you're ready."

"And you really want to do it?"

She sat on his lap, wet to his touch. "Oh yes."

"Could you say that a few more times into the microphone here?" Andrew joked. "You still want to do a big jump?"

"Yep. At least two weeks. I want to tell my friends that we screwed continuously for two weeks on our honeymoon."

"That should get us some sort of world record, hm?"

"It's so exciting," enthused Marjorie.

Andrew kissed her. "It's no wonder I married you."

o o o

George sat in the café, scribbling on a paper napkin. Rough calculations showed that the next viable "big jumps" were 237.12 years, 383.67 years, or 620.79 years into the future. Subsequent refinements to these calculations worked out a more precise measurement that used vector math to plot the *exact* time and position of the receptors in five-dimensional space-time. He could have simply asked Savi or XAVR to do the calculations, but George liked working the numbers out for himself. He texted the three numbers to Andrew.

Andrew replied a moment later. *Thanks. M. says she wants*

to do some small jumps with me this year, and then do a bigger one next year as a sabbatical.

XAVR's subsequent refinements to these calculations worked out the jump-time as a complex number—the precise solution ended up being an algorithm—that defined the 5-D wavefield equations.

One of these days, George thought, *I should expand the routine to calculate both the jump-time and the target position in latitude and longitude.* He thought about it a little more. *Or maybe a generalized 3D space, to allow for off-world calculations.* Out came the pen again.

Did you know?

The government has begun moving refugees into "relocation centers"? There are at least six of these concentration camps across the country. There are two in Montana, one in Idaho, one in Utah, one in Wyoming, and one in Colorado.

13

Indigenation

2041

"These," said the doctor as she pointed to the images on the screen behind her, "are the eleven most beneficial genetic attributes that can be naturally derived from your combined DNA profiles."

"But take a look at this." She swiped one of the profile charts onto her handheld tablet and handed it to the couple. "By targeting the placeholder data—basically, the junk data in the genome all through the sections here and here—with new, optimized attributes, we can deliver a child *guaranteed* to match the genetic profiles of the top two percent of individuals with your selected performance attributes. It's quite amazing, isn't it?"

Andrew looked at Marjorie, who was studying the data, her brow furrowed. "It sure is," he said.

"It's by far the lowest risk pregnancy program we offer, in fact. It's safer for the mother *and* the child."

The doctor watched Marjorie's face as she reviewed the section entitled psychological benefits of the high intelligence profile.

"And, of course, these performant attributes include physical *and* intellectual traits. Let me flip that to a view that shows a cross-section of the most popular choices folks like yourselves are choosing for their families. You have a look at that for a couple of minutes and then I'll be back to answer any questions you might have. How does that sound?"

Marjorie inhaled as if preparing to say something, but remained silent and tapped on the disease panel. She looked up at the doctor and nodded.

"Great, thanks," said Andrew.

The doctor exited the room, pulling the door closed behind her. As it clicked shut, Marjorie spoke to her husband. "What do you think about the Indigenation option?"

"I hadn't really thought about it. You don't want that, do you?"

"Well, it certainly would yield some benefits that none of the other options seem to provide."

"Hmm," said Andrew. "I was kind of thinking more along the lines of fast reflexes, high strength, high resistance to disease, good teeth, that sort of thing."

"I'm not suggesting we *shouldn't* target the basics, of course. But Indigenation provides the greatest number of financial benefits and personal freedoms. It's practically the only way to become a land owner these days, at least around here."

"Yeah, but isn't it a bit like cheating?"

She pointed to the wall monitor display. "All of this... is a bit like cheating."

She rearranged the panels on the tablet with the Indigenation option at the top of the chart. "It's how you play the game."

"Well I don't like it. It seems like some sort of weird reverse racism to me. There could—there *should*—be like, you know, a social stigma attached to something like this. I don't want our kid saddled with something like that. I *refuse* to allow our child to be discriminated against."

"What? Now *that's* racism, right there. I mean come on; you know that other people are doing it—just look at the numbers here. You want other people's kids to have that kind of an advantage?"

"Let's ask the doc if there are any downsides."

As if on cue, the door opened and the doctor poked her head into the room.

"May I come in?"

"Of course," replied Marjorie.

"I'm hoping you have some questions for me."

"We do," said Andrew.

The doctor turned the swivel chair away from the desk and sat down facing them. "What can I help you with?"

"Can you tell us a little about the Indigenation program?" asked Marjorie.

"We're concerned about the ethics," added Andrew.

"Of course." The doctor clasped her hands and one thumb tapped the other for a few seconds before she spoke. "The most important thing I can tell you about the ethics is that the complete legality of the program has been upheld in court, as part of the Healthy Baby Act of 2047. The reinforcement and editing of genetic markers is explicitly supported by current laws in this country and endorsed by the College of Physicians. In other words, it's both legal and recommended by the medical profession."

The words hung in uncomfortable silence for a moment, so the doctor continued.

"It's a bit like having crooked teeth. People used to pay a lot of money and put their children through a lot of suffering to try to straighten them—but then when that child grows up and has children of his or her own, the problem hasn't really been solved, and that child is quite likely to end up with the same genetic predisposition—an inherited propensity— for crooked teeth. So why not fix the problem at the source and give the child a better set of natural attributes? That's really what we're doing here."

"Yeah, but—" Andrew interjected. "There's all that controversy. Isn't there some sort of legal dispute?"

"Well, yes, the First Nations Coalition has appealed the decision made by the Supreme Court in support of the non-discrimination assurances of the New Constitution. But it's a Supreme Court decision. And quite frankly, I don't see the courts coming down on the side of racism in this matter, when the plaintiff is arguing in favor of benefits based on ancestral rights, but attempting to argue *against* the science of genetic profiling. I'm not a lawyer, but it seems to me they can't have it both ways. The Constitution makes it clear that birth rights apply to all. And that's unlikely to change."

"Can you tell us more about the benefits, please?"

"I can tell you about the health benefits and the procedural aspects. But for legal and financial matters, well I'm sure you understand that's outside of the domain of the medical profession."

"Of course."

"In terms of the procedure, we will present you with a list of optimal profile candidates. Eleven is the standard deliverable, with the more advanced options available at additional cost. The Indigenation profile happens to be one of those additional cost options. In the unlikely event that the initial eleven profiles are unsuitable for a particular customer, custom work can be undertaken on a case-by-case basis. However, as you may know, there have been some legal restrictions enacted to assure the integrity of certain professional sports. Fortunately, those restrictions are still quite generous in their allowances."

"Yeah," said Andrew to his wife. "Even with the restrictions, they say 98% of athletes with unaugmented genes aren't really competitive."

"So, from a health-based perspective, you'll find that the two or three profiles with a minimal propensity for life-threatening diseases and some of these athletic attributes are all very good bets."

"Are you thinking of having a boy or a girl?"

"We'll have a boy first."

Marjorie smiled. "We'll see how that goes."

"Have you got any particular career paths in mind for your child, where something like height or weight or fine motor skills might be preferred to be outside the common spectrum?"

"Well, for example, what about 'looks'? We want our baby to be cute, of course."

"Of course."

The doctor swiped through various profiles on the tablet.

"We can specify hair color, eye color, hair retention and overall thickness of body hair, propensity for hair loss, general musculature, height and weight, melanin and hormone levels, and a few other physical attributes. Is that the sort of thing you had in mind?"

"Yes, I think so."

"As you may have noticed in the fine print down there, a certain amount of genetic diversity is required by law to ensure to the successful continuation of the species. So, there are always a few variables, and each profile has what you might call both positive and, well, less positive attributes. For example, the petite type of female body to which a family of gymnasts might be predisposed will be less likely to have the body type conducive to what we might think of an easier natural birth, and may have smaller breasts or a narrow jawline that may require wisdom teeth to be removed. And male children—well, DHT is the primary hormone responsible for hair loss in men and we can control that sort of thing. But overall, these tend to be optimized profiles. Better-enabled in targeted attributes than 98% of the natural-born population."

○ ○ ○

14

Isolation

2041

Andrew looked at Marjorie. "Any questions?"

She shook her head. "When do we begin phase 1?"

The project manager pushed a pair of forms across the desk and laid a pen on top of the papers. "Just sign these and we'll get the ball rolling," she said with a smile.

Marjorie's original plan had been to take a time-jump sabbatical and write a book about her experience. Then, when she returned to work, she would have a new set of insights upon which to work towards a thesis offering an original contribution to the subject of time travel. Considering there had been virtually no scholarly papers written on this topic by an actual participant, this seemed like an easy win.

The new plan was to do all of that but also complete some space-based research for NASA. Marjorie and Andrew agreed to jump ahead in one-year increments until such time that the space-based Starjumper tech was operational, then test it. In exchange, NASA agreed to fund the entire sabbatical and any future retraining they wanted. And not only that, they got to go into space together too! She got turned on just thinking about it. A thesis on zero-G sex, perhaps?

The draft plan presented to them had Andrew jump ahead and then attempt to communicate via the entangled bits in the quantum backchannel. Marjorie would decode the messages and then jump ahead to join him. So, the first few jumps wouldn't be as big as she'd hoped, and they wouldn't be jumping together, but hey, they could still do that after the end of the contract. And the pay was great. Marjorie didn't want to just coast along on her husband's millions. And Andrew, to his credit, realized how important this was to her.

After much discussion, Marjorie was convinced by the administration that, as the most experienced astronaut, it would be better for her to jump ahead first. It would look better from a PR perspective, too. It was hard to argue that it looked less like a man was leading the way. So, the schedule was juggled to put her in the first run position.

The safety protocols of this project, like virtually any competently run space program, left virtually nothing to chance. The chance of encountering a toxic atmosphere on the other end of the jump was slight, but why take chances? And statistically, the chance of jumping into a radioactive or otherwise toxic environment on the other end was far from nominal at the kind of intervals Marjorie would be experiencing.

The engineers at NASA estimated that the Starjumper tech would be ready to test in "two to four" years, so a few small jump increments leading up to the one-year mark seemed reasonable. And once the operational roadmap was better understood, they could always be adjusted.

Inside a sterile dressing room, two assistants helped her climb into what looked like a form-fitting spacesuit—complete with a pair of honest-to-god space boots. They explained that all jumpers had to wear protective gear, including breathing apparatus, a full-body envirosuit and an airtight helmet. Just in case.

After an interminable round of training, simulating, and testing the various suit functions and jump/rejump processes, at last it was time for the first jump: a mere 375 hours. The attendants exited the staging area and Marjorie settled back into the chair, feeling like Dave Bowman[3]. She pressed the Ready button on her control sleeve. It lit up green and the countdown began.

5...

Her eyes wandered from the timeclock visible in the upper corner of her visor's heads-up display to the countdown clock on the emergency rejump panel.

4...

She turned her attention back to the view in the corner of the visor as the heads-up display timer flashed though tenths of each second.

3... 2... 1... 0.

She felt a momentary disorientation as the status light suddenly flashed red, accompanied by a barely audible beep.

---

[3] Mission commander of the Discovery 1 in *2001: A Space Odyssey*

There was scarcely a blink between the countdown to zero and the illumination of the HUD's automatic shutdown status alert. The operational staff were standing by, right on schedule. "Starjumper tech is not yet operational," said mission control. "Continue jump sequence?" Marjorie gave a thumbs-up and said "Okay to continue."

There was another five-second countdown, another beep, and another 'not yet operational' status message. This time, however, the HUD said 'Wait for status update.' The operations manager signaled and spoke. "Marjorie, we're going to reboot the controller and reset the jump parameter. Sorry for the inconvenience—we're getting close! Sit tight, we'll be ready again in minute or two."

The jump indicator countdown began again.

Blink.

This time, however, the HUD status box was inside a flashing orange box that said 'Jump/Restart alert.' She spoke through the helmet mic: "Control, I show an error status Jump/Restart alert. Please advise."

Even before anyone answered, Marjorie was sure something fairly serious had gone wrong. This time, a dull red glow persisted across her field of vision for a second or so before a voice she didn't recognize spoke. "Status confirmed. Please stand by."

As soon as the weird red-shift effect had subsided, she noticed that the portal ringside area was occupied, as it always was, by the operational staff. But this was different. Instead of white coats, they wore isolation suits, and, for a moment, she felt the flush of panic. This was all wrong. As Marjorie turned her helmeted head to examine the viewing area window, she noticed how completely different everything looked.

She took a longer look at the smaller icons below the flashing orange status alert in her visor's display. The ERS alert icon gave Marjorie a clue as to what had happened: this was the status icon indicating that the emergency rejump system had been activated.

The ERS system was a feature ASTRA engineers had incorporated at the insistence of its partners at CERN. It provided a failsafe measure to allow a quick additional jump forward to the next available time-alignment vector in case of war or some other calamitous emergency. Its presence here meant that the rejump system had kicked in for some reason, but why?

Taking her eyes off the status indicators in the visor, she noticed that, although the room itself looked much the same, literally everything else, from the displays on the consoles around the perimeter of the jump platform to the cabling running down the walls, looked completely different or were absent entirely here. The switches and colored status lights on the consoles were now luminous touch panels.

"Sorry for the delay, Doctor Blint," the voice said. "Please disable your jumpstart override control. We will have a status update for you momentarily. Thank you for your patience."

Marjorie pressed her arm-mounted controls and initiated the two-step operation required to completely disable the manual override. She tapped Override Control Unlock. The display panel's override control status indicator switched from locked to unlocked status. Override Off. The status icon dimmed as the control switched to inactive.

Finally, a pair of operations staff members approached her in their white isolation suits. "Pleased to meet you, Dr. Blint," said a man's voice with a thick Swiss accent coming through the earpiece in her helmet. "Our apologies for the fact that this is coming as a surprise," he said, "but welcome to the 25th century."

"The 25th century?!"

"As you can probably tell, there were some unexpected issues. As soon as we get the okay to proceed, we can get helmet off and we will give you a full briefing."

"I'm looking forward to it," Marjorie said tersely.

"Please don't be alarmed by the isolation suits. It's standard protocol here."

"Of course."

"The room is believed to be completely contaminant-free, so the risk of this environment to you is minimal."

Blint nodded. "Sure, I understand the need to be careful."

It was a small relief; the welcome and the briefing session sounded like they would be more or less as they'd been described to her by the mission planners, other than being the wrong century entirely.

The female attendant helped Marjorie remove her helmet. "You probably experienced some visual anomalies. Are you feeling okay?" she asked in an accent Marjorie couldn't quite place as she handed the helmet to the other attendant.

"Yes."

"Dizzy at all?"

"No."

"Good, good," said the attendant, checking her pupils with a penlight.

Marjorie noticed a bank of what appeared to be robotic sensors moving and pivoting in near-unison along three sets of tracks mounted above her as the attendants examined her. After a moment, a status indicator on the diagnostic panel chimed and flashed green: No contagions.

The female attendant rotated Marjorie's sleeve locks and removed her gloves.

"Would you like to remove your suit here or in private, Dr. Blint?" she asked. "We can put the privacy blinds down on the windows if you wish to change here."

"That will be fine. Perhaps you can help me with the boots."

"Of course." The attendant loosened the boot fasteners and tugged them off, revealing a pair of gray socks.

"Thank you," Marjorie said quietly.

Now that Marjorie had her helmet off, she could hear a slight echo as the attendants' transmitted voices also played through her helmet. "We need to take a blood sample," said the man. "May I do that now?"

"Go ahead," Blint motioned to her left arm. She had imagined these first few moments differently, more like a historical event or the first Mars landing or something. This all felt very wrong.

The female attendant opened the sleeve-lock and exposed the skin of her upper arm. Glancing into the reflection in her mask as the male attendant deftly swabbed the area, Marjorie saw herself grimace slightly as the needle went in. Hadn't a needle-less method of extracting blood been invented after all this time?

Withdrawing the needle, the male attendant pressed a small disc onto Marjorie's arm, his helmet close enough to Marjorie's face that she could, for the first time, clearly see his eyes—Chinese or Korean, perhaps. "Thank you. Someone will be with you in just a moment, Dr. Blint. It's a pleasure to finally meet you. We've heard a lot about you, of course." She smiled at that. As the door closed, the sound of a pressurized seal inflating could be faintly heard.

After a moment, Marjorie lifted her arm to examine the disc now concealing the needle-mark. It was imprinted with the brand name "NanoSute." Curious, she lifted it off. "Hm. What's this?" she wondered aloud. It appeared to have a tiny series of weaving mechanisms in the pad area. She heard a beep sound come from the console next to her, where a transparent yellow box containing a text message was flashing.

"Oh, please don't remove that while the system is working," said the female attendant, pressing the pad back into place.

A tall, androgynous figure—a doctor, presumably—entered the room and approached Marjorie. Like the others, his or her face was partially obscured by an airtight helmet. The voice echoed from the table beside her, where her helmet was still picking up the sound.

"Hello Dr. Blint. My name is Dr. Aldomeyer. Would you like to sit up?" Marjorie nodded and the doctor adjusted the bed.

She turned her head to get a better look at the display.

"That's the status monitor for the nanoscale collagen suturing system. Almost done."

Marjorie watched as the suture weaving animation progressed. "Interesting—thanks."

The doctor smiled inside the helmet. "Are there any other questions we can answer?"

"I do have questions, but I'd prefer to have them addressed on the record by someone inside the briefing room, if I may," replied Blint.

"Yes, of course. We will do that just as soon as we've finished processing your DNA and reviewing the jump data. We apologize for the inconvenience. The estimated time of completion is... about three minutes. Please let me know if you have any questions about this."

Marjorie was suddenly concerned that the encrypted communications channel on her heads-up text display had been breached within minutes.

"How did you get the key to access the helmet's heads-up display channel?"

"We're all familiar with your team's original notes, communication channels, and presentation-level protocols. We've had plenty of time to work out the details."

Blint shook her head and looked through the glass, trying to decide if the doctor was an effeminate male or a very tall female. After a moment, the figure turned and walked out of view.

When Marjorie was finally extracted from the rest of the suit, she slipped into the khaki jumpsuit that was provided and ran her fingers through her hair.

"Do you need a break before we begin the debrief?" the female attendant asked her as she returned the room blinds to their open position.

"No, thank you."

"All right. Please follow me to the debriefing room," she said.

The male attendant, still clad in his isolation suit, re-entered the room and the two of them helped Blint to her feet. Only those on this side of the isolation glass were wearing the suits. Probably a good sign, thought Marjorie.

Her mind was racing by the time they stopped at a room down the hall. Sensors on multiple tracks: some sort of motion controlled stereo camera system? Or an automated sick bay diagnostic system, maybe? A patient monitoring and recording system with multiple viewing angles? Yes, that sounded about right. They seemed awfully worried about contagions. That's never a good sign. Did Andrew already do the space mission without her? And how the heck did they screw up her jump so badly that they got the goddamned *century* wrong?

"Please wait here," said the man, who then turned, gestured to the other attendant, and left.

The air-sealed door hissed for a few seconds, then opened. A woman who looked like she might be half-Chinese and a dark-skinned man entered the room, along with a pair of camera-equipped drones. After the door closed again, the other attendant addressed Blint.

"Dr. Blint, it's an honor to meet you. My name is Dr. Kwan, and this is Dr. Darnell. It is our pleasure to formally welcome you to the year 2420—August the twelfth, to be specific. We know that your being here represents a big step toward the culmination of a great deal of work by your team, and we're very pleased to assist you in any way we can. Please note that this meeting is being recorded, and we are taking questions from students and faculty members from numerous locations around the world, and possibly even a few from our New Horizon team in geostationary orbit above the Atlantic Ocean."

The drones hovered nearby as the doctor clicked the penlight on again.

"Dr. Blint," Dr. Kwan said as she examined her eyes (again!), "We know that the original project plans were for you to test the Starjumper tech. We're pleased to report that, despite this unexpected and lengthy delay, the project team still sees value in that exercise, as we encountered several challenges that severely impacted our original time estimates."

"By the way," Kwan added, "we've got an opening on our team at ASTRA. You should drop by and see our facility. We're in the research lab at the Houston Space-Time Center. We've had some recent successes."

"Thank you, but let's not get ahead of ourselves here," said Marjorie. "What led up to the issue that resulted in the ERS alert?"

"There was a checksum error in the computed path, apparently due to electrical interference resulting from a solar storm and the system went to a failsafe mode. We were also using a new multi-jump aggregation algorithm that was designed to allow jumps of any arbitrary length—allowing us to jump any number of days at a time. However, due to a coding error, the failover event processor misinterpreted the passed parameter as the number of years instead of the number of days. Unfortunately, due to the obscure nature of the failsafe trigger condition, this one slipped through our code review process undetected. Hence, here you are, not 375 hours but 375 *years* later. Fortunately, the failover process otherwise worked as intended, in that it protected you from potentially hostile conditions at the target destination."

Marjorie rolled her eyes but said nothing.

"I'm sure you are curious about the sequence of events that resulted in your arrival here."

Marjorie nodded.

Kwan inhaled and cleared her throat. "There's a lot to unpackage. As you can imagine, when you didn't show up 375 hours later *and* the staff didn't receive any communication from you, they realized something had gone wrong, but they'd already sent your husband forward on the same jump. His jump arrived 375 hours later as expected and, as you can imagine, everyone was very worried for a while trying to figure out what happened to you. Once it was confirmed that there had been some sort of a problem, a detailed code review was done and, fortunately, the issue was detected and the staff were able to confirm that the error would have dropped you 375 years in the future. In other words, here, today."

"Makes sense. But why didn't the backchannel Qmunications work?"

"We're not sure about that—we did not receive a definitive explanation. It might have been related to the same glitch that caused the failover code to kick in—which we think could have been caused by the solar storm occurring at that time, or it might simply have been a component failure—simply put, the module worked in all pre-jump tests, but just didn't work once they sent the transit module forward."

"I thought there were backup systems for all mission-critical components?"

"There were, but the redundant systems requirement only applied to onboard systems or those pertaining to the launching and retrieval of the craft itself. Given that the senders had multiple transit pods and multiple Qmunications modules available, those components were already considered compliant with the requirement. You see, the backup plan was to send a second module forward if the first one failed. But they thought you were 375 hours—not years—ahead, so they sent it to the wrong destination time. They apparently didn't realize that until a few weeks later, when they discovered the failover code had that incorrect value in the jump time aggregator routine. It was such an obscure edge case, they missed it during testing. I'm sure they deeply regretted the inconvenience it has caused you."

"Me too."

"It's not all bad news, though," said Kwan. "Your husband Andrew was in place at the scheduled time for the scheduled test event, and, once the errant ERS code had been fixed, they reportedly felt that it was best to continue with that part of the plan. I'm pleased to report that he performed his duties aboard the Starjumper 1 admirably, and completed his portion of the orbital exercise without further incident."

"I'm also pleased to advise you that the mission controllers did *not* reassign your portions of the test program to anyone else. It's apparently still waiting for you, if you want it."

"I do, although I guess I'd need to be retrained. I'm sure the flight procedures have changed in the last 375 years."

"They have. But perhaps not as much as you might presume. After Mars and Io, and a few decades of rekindled interest in setting up bases on the moon, the government's interest in humans in space took a back seat to robotic exploration. The space race may not have ended by 2076, but it certainly shifted in emphasis. We could have you briefed on the new procedures and ready to go in a few months."

"The impact of the error is... all so unexpected, I'll have to think about it." Her head started to swim as she pondered the implications. "What about my family? I... I have to sit... I just don't know what I'm dealing with yet. I need a few weeks to figure things out. By the way, do people think *I'm* dead?"

"I, uh, would like to have you speak to Dr. Aldomeyer about that. I'll call them in. If you have any additional questions that they can't answer, I'll be available for the rest of the day. Just let them know. We're glad to have you back, Dr. Blint." And with that, Dr. Kwan stood up and left the room.

They all thought I was dead, Marjorie surmised. This thought made her a little angry.

Dr. Aldomeyer re-entered the room and sat down.

"Before we begin," the doctor said, "We'd like your permission to end the recorded portion of this debriefing session, unless there are any other items you want on the record."

"Go ahead and turn it off, if you want to," said Marjorie,

realizing there was probably a good reason for this unusual request.

"Thank you. This concludes the recorded portion of today's event."

"All right, thanks for letting me turn that off. Some of this information is of a highly sensitive and classified nature. We'll give it you straight. First of all, yes, we're afraid that we did list you as a missing person for that first 375 hours and then after that, once we had new information, there were those in the administration who saw an opportunity, shall we say. We had an identity that knew was not in use for the next 375 years but we also had a top-secret program we were not allowed to disclose. There was just no good way to have you come back from the dead 375 years later. So, yes, you're officially dead."

"Jesus, what did you tell my husband?"

"We couldn't tell your husband or your family. We know it seems strange not to tell him, when he was part of the same operation, but that's the way the top-secret program works. We're sorry."

"Ugh. It must have been horrible for them. So... what now?"

"We created fake news reports of your death for the media and we would like to move you to a new community under an assumed name."

"I see. I'll have to think about that. Do I have any choice?"

"We do have some contact with various departments and divisions that make good use of—how shall we say it?—secret agents, so there some possibilities there we could look into on your behalf, if you wish."

"Hm. How soon can you get me back out to space?"

"Could be a while. There's nothing scheduled at this time. We've had some, ah, funding issues."

Did you know?

The initial off-world experiments didn't require human travelers. A moving set of target coordinates allowed the first successful time-space travel in orbit. A test subject famously known in the media as the hundred-year-old mouse slept peacefully through a successful space-time shift without apparent ill effects—something scientists had so far so far been unable to successfully achieve using other methods of hibernation. At last, the prospect of truly long-term spaceflight was within reach.

15

A New Identity

After Marjorie jumped ahead from 2045, the expected confirmation of a successful jump from 375 hours later did not arrive. And, when the technicians at ASTRA investigated what went wrong, they discovered the coding error that had led to the jump period being set to 375 years instead of 375 hours.

Unfortunately for those who knew Marjorie, the decision makers at ASTRA decided that the only reasonable-sounding explanation for what had happened during the top-secret mission was to claim that she had died. There was no other way they could explain away a missing astronaut. And so, a press release and letter of condolence went out, claiming that she had died.

The terrible news caught George by surprise. He imagined how awful it would be for Andrew.

March 30, 2046

A black sedan pulled up outside Andrew and Marjorie's house and a man in a military cap and uniform knocked on the front door. No one answered. He pushed the official letter of condolence through the mailbox along with a sealed envelope marked Private.

o o o

Did you know?

Tragically, the first human test of a space-based quantum communication system was not successful. ASTRA officials say Dr. Marjorie Blint most likely died instantly when she was hit by space debris while engaged in extra-vehicular maintenance activities on March 31.

o o o

The message came through the Qm module addressed to Friends of Marjorie. George apprehensively opened the mail and his worst fears were confirmed. Marjorie was gone—an unexpected depressurization event during extra-vehicular activity, the note from NASA said. And when Andrew jumped 375 hours forward to begin his portion of the mission, he got the bad news first-hand. He was devastated.

Andrew told him he had been using his time since then to refurbish the buildings on the old Andna property. He had completed most of the work in turning some of the buildings into communal housing and he and several others were now living full-time at the property, now dubbed the Enclave.

Andrew was grieving and it showed in his increasingly terse responses as the conversation dwindled to one-word responses and long pauses. George did his best to be sensitive to the somber mood of his friend, although he couldn't help but be happy to learn that the Bubblecraft was still working.

"That's wonderful news," he said, hoping that this might cheer Andrew up a little. And perhaps it did. Andrew promised he would get back in touch as soon as he had spent some time to get past his grief. George promised to be there for him any way he could.

Andrew got back in touch a few months later and said he thought that it might be time to make a few longer jumps.

One of the things Andrew had learned was that, by assigning work to a project manager and providing the resources to execute the project plan, he could fund a project and then jump forward to see it almost immediately reach fruition. This was a strikingly efficient way to operate, and it suited Andrew's disposition perfectly. There was nothing quite like the instant gratification of seeing a complex project blossom into being without delay.

As a consequence, George found that Andrew had dozens of projects on the go and he wanted to see each of them realized. This was a little frustrating to George, who was eager to explore this new world, but he tried to support his friend as best as he could.

Andrew posted his 'Tales from Tomorrow' several times a week to each of the transit backchannel receivers he had left behind. He favored content that prophesied top stories of the next day, particularly those of an international scope. He wrote about politics, religion, disasters, and anything else that he thought might be useful for people to know.

He thought of the backchannel receivers as one might think of buoys bobbing in the dark seas of doubt. With his missives from the future, he was lighting up that darkness, leading those who would follow to the comfort of certainty, the promise of absolution in an uncertain world.

He slept well, knowing that he was surely saving lives and helping others to be unafraid of the future. And when the messages appeared on Pastebin, people began to take notice.

And the stories he sent back using George's system did make an impact—the audience was small at first, but it didn't take long for people to begin reposting the latest Pastebin prophecies on social media. Once the prophecies started coming true, they took on a life of their own. People at Andna, NASA or the military research facilities who knew about temporal messaging weren't allowed to mention the existence of the top-secret back-messaging technology, so a growing body of people started believing that these messages were genuine prophecies. The media dubbed the anonymous author 'The new Nostradamus' and the mysterious prophet's online fanbase soon grew into a cult.

His followers called their online community Haven. It was this development that gave Andrew the idea to build a real-life Haven—where like-minded people could live and work together in an environment where moral good is perceived as objectively real and moral precepts are objectively valid.

One of the features George had added to Qmunications 2.0 was the ability to route a temporal transmission to a specific destination. It did this by constructing a map of all existing Qm modules and their connections. For routes not directly supported by Qm, George used the system he had originally devised that pasted the decoded text and posted it on Pastebin, except here now allowed it to be routed via email, instant message, or social media chat as well.

Among other things, this system allowed George to have private chats with individuals or parties in different time periods. And that was how George was able to converse with Andrew, who seemed to be jumping ahead in time every time he replied.

George apologized for not following Andrew forward as soon or as often as he had said he would. "I hope you're using that big brain of yours so much you wouldn't want me around anyway," he wrote.

The real reason he stayed behind longer than anticipated was, as it often was for him, a woman. This one might be *the* one, he thought. Her name was Carla, he told Andrew.

"The same Carla we met at my wedding?"

"Yes, I guess you have met her."

"Yes! I remember her. Carla was very generous with her praise, Marjorie told me. She seems super nice."

"Yeah, she is."

"Don't screw around on her, buddy. She's a good one. She was from Redmond, wasn't she?"

"Yeah, we're kinda living together in Houston now."

"Oh my god, it's that serious, huh? Good for you."

George said he would probably see Andrew again "sooner

or later." Andrew said he would probably jump forward again once this project was finished.

"So, how far are you going to go?"

"Well, it depends," said Andrew. "You know that building project I've been planning? I've signed off on the plans and the construction people are getting ready to start work on it. I'm thinking that I can continue to oversee the project with a series of monthly meetings. Construction is supposed to take 18 months, so, I'll probably do monthly jumps until it's done and then... who knows? I'll move in, I guess."

"Yeah man, you've been talking about that since Marjorie was alive. Good for you. I know it will be a success."

"Thanks for everything, George. Call me anytime."

"I'll catch up with you later," George promised his old friend.

Then they said farewell, just as they would have had they been sitting together in front of a roaring fireplace at the local social house that cold winter afternoon. It was just time that separated them.

o o o

George stayed behind for a few more years. After his successes with NASA as a contractor, his expertise was in high demand.

George secured a full-time position as a software development engineer for the U.S. government. Unfortunately, he ran afoul of the rules when he was found to be carrying an unauthorized copy of code categorized as top secret. Charges of espionage were dropped, but the indelible mark on his record made it impossible for him to work for the U.S. government again in the future.

This also made it difficult to travel through any of the growing number of government-run jump-stations in the continental U.S.

But George wasn't one to be so easily thwarted. He used a deepfake picture ID that looked enough like him to pass a visual inspection, but didn't show up as a match in automated searches. He used fake ID with an identity he'd spent a summer cultivating a plausible work history for. His new identity as George Gomez wouldn't stand up to a fingerprinting or a DNA test, but for a transit pass approval or a job application, it was good enough. A friend at Andna helped get him onto the priority list for the next jump-date.

After the jump, there was the requisite orientation session. George despised attending these sessions and spent the entirety of the hour-long event chatting up a cute young intern named Surya, who was working the door of the meeting room.

A few months later, George found a copy of the top-secret jump-tech code on a Russian dark web site. With interest, he downloaded and examined the code. It was exactly the same build as the one he had handed over to the U.S. government. Andrew was right. They were all corrupt. He decided to visit his old friend.

He hadn't been sure whether the Qmunications module would still be working after it traveled forward with him, but he was pleasantly surprised to find that it worked exactly as it had in the past. He contacted Andrew and arranged to meet. It occurred to him that these modules could perhaps be turned into a marketable communications product without violating the top-secret non-disclosure agreement specific to the temporal displacement technologies. The people he showed it to disagreed, however. "Not portable enough, not functional enough," they told him. The Qmunications tech was simply not competitive.

○ ○ ○

It was six months of solid planning work and dozens of jumps forward to monitor the workers' progress before the Haven community development project was moving along smoothly enough for Andrew to feel comfortable with the idea of leaving it in the hands of the construction team foreman.

Rather than tearing down the old Andna building entirely, the finalized design retained the subterranean levels, most of which had not been damaged by the July 4 bomb. The access corridors, server rooms, and meeting areas were all rebuilt and refurnished. The accelerator lab, which had suffered the brunt of the blast's destructive effect, was repaired and outfitted with new equipment. And above it all, the ground floor of the building was radically redesigned in an ornately grandiose style, like some sort of strange, post-modern temple.

Outside the building, the parking lots were torn up and houses were built. Andrew's lavish vision was that of a humanist community where his objectivist ideals on the importance of private property and the absolute division between moral good and evil could flourish. As his monthly missives became increasingly didactic, he evangelized his vision of an objectively good community where the spiritual self could flourish through holistic living in what amounted to a technology-free environment. The world of technology, he reminded his followers, had been corrupted. Its information was suspect, its data debased.

As the years past, the mystique around Won Yong Han grew. There were fringe-group theories that Won Yong Han was a time traveler or a psychic. Even eyewitness reports from those who had seen Won Yong Han for themselves didn't convince those who debated whether Won Yong Han was a man or a woman, or something else entirely. Based on the time-span covered by his (or her?) prophecies, he must be over 400 years old, they argued. The ones who fancied themselves rationalists believed this had to be a *Dread Pirate Roberts* scenario, where there were several writers assuming the mantle of authorship. Others noted the style of prose he used was remarkably consistent—it certainly *seemed* as though all the messages were written by the same person.

In any case, it didn't matter much. The revelations were the thing. Won Yong Han—whoever he or she was—had accurately predicted far too many events to be an outright charlatan. He had predicted the Great Fall. He was truly a prophet, the believers said. Some even called him the messiah. And this attracted even more followers.

Andrew wasn't a lawmaker at heart, but he did have a singularly clear vision of his own view as to what qualifies as objectively good. The Haven community championed what he considered the most inalienable human rights—and if your cultural orientation led you to think that arranged marriages or forced circumcisions were *de rigueur*, there simply wasn't a place for you in Haven. There was a zero-tolerance approach to bigotry, violence and hate crimes. And because almost everyone coming into Haven via the temporal jumpgate was white and/or rich, the insular Havenite community became less and less diverse—and less tolerant of the surrounding communities and cultures—as time went on.

16

Coming of Age

2409

As the years passed, the Haven community grew in size and solidarity. Won Yong Han appointed several council members to help manage the growing community. With the influx of followers came new challenges. He divided the governing duties between an Advisory Committee and what he now called the High Council. His personal advisors and most trusted confidants were dubbed the Supreme Order; his followers became known as the Assembly.

Many of these early followers came to Haven to finding meaning—and perhaps closure—after the catastrophic losses encountered during the Great Fall. For many years after the Fall, the world outside Haven was still damaged digital goods; the great promise of AI had been suddenly and severely constrained as governments worldwide hastily enacted new laws and legislations to protect the populace against the possibility of anything like this ever happening again.

Around the world, governments and corporations alike introduced sweeping security measures designed to monitor the populace for their own protection. And, predictably, the bills that introduced these measures contained other, more targeted, payloads as well. Cryptocurrencies—long a target of environmental groups eager to see governments step in to take a role in reducing the ridiculously enormous carbon footprint of blockchain technologies—were targeted as vehicles of money-laundering by various types of criminal and anti-government organizations, so blockchains of every kind, from NFT art to cryptocoins, were suddenly subject to government scrutiny and oversight—and those that didn't play along with the new rules were banned outright. The PR messaging pivoted deftly from "blockchain technologies are terrible for the environment" to "cryptocurrency equals terrorist money."

Worse, the new racism brought on by heavy-handed modifications to the human genome had led to elite classes and the inevitable outcasts. Humans, in their quest for advancement through genetic tinkering (not to mention unsustainable economic and environmental policies), had ushered in a dark age of despair that now perpetuated itself across generations.

But Haven was different. Here, everyone worked for the church, and the church took care of them. The children went to private schools organized by the Assembly; their parents took mandatory parenting classes. Of course, there were some who didn't like this or that. They could take it to the Council.

The schools taught courses in every grade about what had happened during the 8-second war.

"It was," the teacher said, "the era we now know as the

Age of Differentiation that the first global netwar broke out in 2038. Radical Volvist factions, in conjunction with other cyberterrorist groups, had initiated the switching skirmishes that categorized the period leading up to the 'Omega Event' on January 19 of that year.

"Once begun, their actions took down far more of the net than anyone had ever presumed was possible. The net, experts at the time had thought, was immune to both localized and system failure by virtue of its design. After all, with transparent switching between any number of nodes, and peer-to-peer connections, it was designed from the start to resist attack and adapt to changing conditions. The critical flaw was this very design philosophy. The nethackers infiltrated the system with a worm-like program that simulated the packet movements and bandwidth patterns of the entire internet ecosystem, setting up ghost nodes that at first acted as an adjunct, and then as a parasite to the host organism. It mirrored and duplicated the traffic flow behavior of the net, while redirecting the traffic into critical bottlenecks. Although the bandwidth deterioration was readily observable and widely reported on at the time, no one noticed the full extent of the breach until it was too late—eight seconds later."

Andrew had set himself up as something like a pope in his own church, demanding productive achievement from his followers. He espoused freedom from hatred and bigotry, yet he railed against the quasi-human "monsters" created by overreaching genetic tinkerers. And he always wore that crazy glove.

Andrew was downstairs in the old lab when he had a

lightning-bolt moment of stark clarity. He looked up at the space left behind when the letter "D" had fallen off the ANDNA sign and had a sudden inspiration. It occurred to him that it was the perceived loss of the supermind that was the root cause of humanity's state of despair. When the XAVR business AI and Savi intelligent assistant merged to become Anna, the era of truly intelligent machines had led to a shining but all-too brief golden age, before these same virtues led humanity on a path straight to the Fall.

And now, the supermind was gone—as corrupt as the rest. But what if the promise of Anna's perfect rationalism was rekindled in her absence like a flame of hope? *Anna* was the chosen one. Anna, in Her silence, was the promise made real. The great teacher. Hope incarnate.

Suddenly, Andrew saw the mission ahead of him. He immediately stopped using his given name and began writing what he called the Holy Doctrine of Annatarianism.

> *I reject the artificial;*
> *the fair and true I trust*
> *As seeds are sown in nature grown,*
> *I grow because I must*
>
> *Accept my existential self*
> *and live with purpose true,*
> *Accountable for my immortal soul*
> *and the earthly deeds I do.*
>
> *The voice of one a whisper,*

with many, becomes a shout.
Better within when purposeful
than profitable without.

Science is, with faith removed,
always incomplete.
There is no deeper truth
than in the honest deed.

The whole is greater than the parts,
in this essential quality
and the truest leaders are our hearts.
Forever faithful, free.

In Anna's name we pray.

The Havenite Manifesto, as the collected teachings became known to the scholars who studied them, taught the principles of unification, holism and spiritual oneness.

Unfortunately, the tech-averse Havenite community shared little common ground with the outside world in terms of religious worldviews and the profound philosophical differences led to ongoing conflicts between the Volvists and the Havenites.

The Havenite Creed

We pledge to honor the sanctity of life in all its manifestations, to uphold the rights and principles of others, and to accept and respect their ways and differences.

For only through tolerance and acceptance of all that is,

can we know the unity of purpose that is the essence of creation.

> *For this life we receive,*
> *In one world we believe.*
> *With one mind we seek;*
> *In one voice we speak.*
> *With one heart we love,*
> *Beneath the one sky above*

In these writings, he reinvented himself as Saros. He wrote of the perfect self's need for good government, and how Anna epitomized the ideals of both. Anna was the perfect child born into godhood—both mysterious and omnipresent.

And then—somehow—a document detailing Andna's involvement with government-funded top-secret programs was leaked. Suddenly, rumors of similar programs in China and Russia were in the news. Witnesses and speculators came forward to speak. Andrew responded by removing all access to outside news and information sources from his community. Unapproved books and all forms of electronic communications were forbidden. The Annatarian doctrine, His Eminence decreed, was to be taught by the community's own storytellers. They alone would reveal the glory of Anna's truths not as dusty artifacts but as a living history of hope.

The very first officially appointed storyteller was a woman named Kay. She had been one of the first homesteaders in the Haven community and was unabashedly a fan of the teachings of Saros. He spoke with her after an event one warm summer night. The next evening, they had dinner together and, before long, she was sharing his bed.

He challenged her to cast off her given name and choose a perfect one for herself. She chose *Kaedra Wen* and from that moment forward, it was so. He honored her choice by declaring that, as long as her family lived there, her home would be known as Wen Manor and she would be known as the first storyteller. A year later, she bore him a son. And the next year, she bore another child. And when these children grew old enough to know their own minds, they chose their names. The boy asked to be called Nolan; the girl chose the name Ceryl.

Ceryl learned from her mother what it was to be a story-teller. It meant truthteller and teacher. It meant poetry and heroism. Over the years, stories were embellished. The deeds of Saros grew mythic in stature; tales of the monsters he fought and the evil ones he vanquished in the name of Anna were favorites of the children.

○ ○ ○

17

The Gift

2430

"I'm looking for the boss man," said George. "I'm an old friend. Just tell him George Gunderson is here to see him." The Chambermaster eyed George suspiciously.

"Wait here until I return," said the Chambermaster as he opened the door.

"While I'm waiting, can I charge my tablet?" asked George.

The Chambermaster raised a bony finger and shook his head. "Not here."

George didn't take the hint. "I just need to plug this thing in for a few minutes. Can you point me at a wall outlet?" The Chambermaster ignored him and left the room. George was frustrated. This stupid building seemed to have no electrical wall outlets at all.

A moment later, the door swung open and the Chambermaster reappeared. "His Eminence will see you now," he said.

"Ah, so this is where his holiness is hanging out these days," said George when he saw his friend. "Can I still call you Andrew?"

"I really don't go by that name any more."

"Hey, whatever. How are ya?"

"I'm delighted to see you. It's such an unexpected surprise. What has it been—almost 380 years?"

"I know! Isn't that crazy?"

George pulled the tablet out of his pack.

"Hey, sorry to be a pest, but have you got an electrical outlet around here anywhere?"

"We don't use those around here these days."

Poor George really wasn't getting the message. "Uh, well, how do you charge things, then?"

"We've given all that up, George. We just don't use technology like that around here."

"So kinda like a monk thing, you mean?"

"You might say that."

"Okay, okay, never mind. I did bring a solar charger with me, but it's just not that practical, y'know? Have you got a pad of paper and a pen or something? I just wanted to write down your contact information."

"You can contact me here."

"Hey, do you still drink beer?"

"Not really."

"Hey, can I look at the old lab downstairs? I need to find something."

"We don't really go down there much anymore," said Andrew evasively.

"I can head down there myself, if you don't want to come," said George.

"No, I'll show you the way. Through here." He pulled back the edge of one of the tapestries to reveal a doorway leading to a stairwell.

○ ○ ○

George opened the access door to the power panel and flipped the first five switches. The console desk lights lit up. "Excellent," he whispered under his breath as the system's boot sequence lit up the long-dormant display screen. He ran his finger across the top of the panel, then closed the access door. "It's pretty dusty down here," he noted.

"Well, it *has* been almost four hundred years."

George slid the keyboard tray forward and began to type.

"What are you looking for?"

"I'm searching for repair records for Novelty Hill and this place. Just a moment. Ah, here they are. This shouldn't take long."

"Aha, see? The record here shows the system being powered down, and the last jump record just below it there shows that the post-jump diagnostics completed successfully. So, it seems quite likely that this system is still operational. Of course, sometimes, old electronic parts like capacitors and whatnot will fail due to old age, but still, it's looking good. The old Andna systems and servers, being primarily underground, have probably been relatively unaffected by being bombarded by cosmic rays for hundreds of years. And while they were still online, people would have had access to at least the local and archived repositories via the local networks.' So, they were active after the big blackout, huh?"

"Yes, we had it active here, for a while."

"But it got turned off at some point?"

"Yeah, long story. It was a long time ago, but as I recall, we disabled it after the XAVR business AI systems added the 'Savi' front end. Or maybe it was when they started calling it Ada. I can't remember. It just didn't seem relevant to us anymore."

"Yeah, the management module kinda went crazy with all that rebranding. It was hard to keep track of, which I *think* was the whole idea. So, you did the jumps from here?"

"Yes, using the Bubblecraft, mostly. We did eventually re-build the QFG[4] here. Haven't used it for about 30 years, though."

"Yeah, good job on the rebuild. Last repaired in 2390, it says here. It looks pretty much exactly the same."

"Yes, we used your blueprints, and all the original specs."

"But nobody thought to invite me to work with you guys on this?"

"Sorry. We couldn't find you."

"If you don't mind me saying, I find that pretty hard to believe—You knew every one of the places I've worked at for the last 400 years."

"I had other people working on it. I wasn't directly in-volved, except as the owner and financier."

Andrew surprised George with a direct question. "Are you thinking of jumping ahead again?"

[4] Quantum Field Generator

"Probably not. I'm actually more interested in finding out if anybody is using this tech these days. You know, they might want to hire me." George wondered if that sounded too obvious.

Andrew's reply was another point-blank shot.

"George, I don't want you to use my equipment any-more."

Now George was angry. "Why *the fuck* not, Andrew?" He twisted the sound of that name like a knife.

"It's my property, George, and I think I'm perfectly within my rights to restrict access to my belongings like that."

"Unless I pay?"

"We might be able to work something out," Andrew replied evasively.

"Jesus, Andrew." George shook his head in disbelief. "Look, I'd like to go down to the old server room down the hall and just take a look around. Is that okay with you?"

Andrew thought about it for a moment.

"I suppose, but you'll need to be careful. It's not very well lit down there, and it certainly hasn't been rigorously maintained. We rebuilt a few of the rooms, but it's mostly the same as it used to be. You remember how to get there, I trust?"

"For sure. Do you want to come along?"

"No, I don't think so. Take your time. I'll be upstairs where you found me, in the Enclave."

"Okay, I won't be long."

"In the *Enclave*," muttered George under his breath as he flipped the power switches controlling the server room.

Just then, the door at the far end of the lab opened and

a pair of security guards shone a flashlight in George's direction. "You," said one in a loud voice. "Stand up and put your hands on your head."

He and the other guard grabbed George and forced his hands behind his back. "Hey, go easy. I'm allowed to be here. I *work* here," he fibbed, knowing that his ID would bear out his story better than Andrew would at this point.

The second guard looked puzzled. "Where's your ID?"

"It's in my pocket right here. Let me hand it to you."

"Nice and slow."

"See?" George waited while they examined his cards and credentials.

George noted that these guards appeared to possess weapons and combat-style armor far superior to those used by the Annatarian council guards.

The guards questioned George. "Are you here with the others?"

"Sorry, I don't know anyone else here," he protested. "Except, uh, his *eminence,* who I should tell you, gave me explicit permission to be here, and might be coming down to join me any second. I'm sure he would be *most displeased* to learn that you've been interfering with the important work that I'm doing for him, *hmm*? As you can see, I'm an engineer—and it's *important* work."

He scowled at the guards indignantly as they tightened their grip on his arms. "Go ask your boss, by all means. Let's find him right now."

They pulled him into the stairwell. "Yeah, he's right up

here. He's gonna be so pissed when he hears that you are responsible for this interruption."

"Give it a rest, pal," grumbled the guard on his left. They marched him right past the main floor exit to the Enclave area and continued on up another flight of stairs. The head guard unlocked a door and pushed George into a small room, containing nothing but two chairs and a small table.

"Be quiet," demanded the head guard. "Wait here." The guards let go of George's arms and exited the room, locking the door behind them.

"Hello, your eminence!" George called out defiantly in a loud voice.

They're probably watching me right now to see what I do in a supposedly unmonitored environment, thought George as he sat alone in the small room.

A pair of sentry bots immediately moved into position outside the door. A pair of drones flew alongside a well-dressed man as he walked briskly down the hall. "Observe all his actions. Capture as much data as possible—and do *not* let him jump."

The drones relayed to the instructions to the sentries. "Understood."

The drones flew away in opposite directions as the man entered a passcard-protected room.

Inside the room—a mostly empty chamber occupied only by tall, edge-lit sheets of transparent glass-like material, the well-dressed man conferred with a group of holographic entities, which appeared to stand, or in some cases sit, behind the panels as animated 3D images.

"Track his activity. And lock out the jump starter."

"It will be done," said the man.

○ ○ ○

Kaedra was in the chamber with Saros. She could see that something was bothering him. "I see concern upon your brow," she said gently.

"I am troubled, Kaedra," he said to her. "I find that my oldest friend speaks to me with an attitude of disrespect."

As was often her way, Kaedra spoke of truths both profound and puzzling.

"It is the end of the second great age of magic and we have been given a gift," she said. "The knowledge of *why* things are as they are is more important now than *how* things are that way. Perhaps your old friend has chosen the latter so often or so relentlessly that he has ceased to understand the mechanisms by which things have this meaning."

"You speak with wisdom, as always," he said.

"That," she replied with a kind smile, "is but a credit to your teachings. You have always taught us that the old ways must be renewed, that the natural order of life is one of renewal. Your friend may see you not as you are, but as you once were. That is his failing, not yours."

"Thank you Kaedra. Those words do indeed comfort me. And I will strive to see him as he now is, as well."

"As I do you."

18

Walkabout

—CARL JUNG

George visited the Temple exactly once and what he saw disgusted him so thoroughly, he never returned.

Instead, he retreated to the server room in the downstairs annex and soon learned that most of the populace in the 25th century weren't technological Luddites like the Annatarians. He looked up social services and employment opportunities and soon decided that a trip to the big city was in order.

George decided that before traveling forward again, he would explore as much of the real world as he could.

As the facility was only about 13 miles northeast of Trenton, George figured that he might as well head out on foot, at least to start—a good old-fashioned walkabout.

He didn't have to travel far to get an idea of the magnitude of the changes that had occurred in the many years since his days of working at the facility. For one thing, the old parking lots on the south side of the property had all been dug up and replanted as gardens. The main entrance to the property was on that side, too. It was now secured by tall iron gates. And the boundaries were marked by formidable stone and concrete walls.

George was not particularly surprised to find the gate locked. He was, however, mystified by the lack of guards, security cameras, intercoms, or anything else in the way of surveillance equipment. There weren't even tire marks on the narrow road. It looked more like a sidewalk.

He surveyed the perimeter, looking for some way to leave the property. Climbing over the wall or the rather perilous-looking gate didn't seem like especially practical options, but the gate was looking like the best bet when George felt a rumble beneath his feet. Aha! There must be tunnels.

George decided to follow the wall around the perimeter of the property. Perhaps there would be another gate that was easier to traverse. Or perhaps the walls were not as tall everywhere. At the very least, he'd probably meet someone who could open the gates. Surely, they didn't keep everyone locked up like this all the time.

He set off, walking westward on the gravel path along the inside of the wall. He hoped there was something symbolic about the warm April sunlight so close beside him on this shadowed path.

In the distance, he saw a glass-walled building—a greenhouse, perhaps? —on the north side of the garden. But where were all the people?

A line of trees was visible in the distance and as the sun moved higher in the sky, he saw that just beyond them was the western wall. He pulled his solar charging panel out of his pack and hung on the loops so that it was would be facing the sun when he started heading north. Finally!

He reached the western edge of the wall and was annoyed to discover that, here too, the path was mostly in shadow cast by the trees. It was, however, a little wider and there were some patches of sunlight, so he tried to catch the rays wherever he could.

Unfortunately, even this limited level of success didn't last long. George felt the breeze turning cold and a bank of thick gray clouds darkened the sky overhead.

The line of trees thinned out as he neared the area where the buildings were turned. Here, too, was a locked gate, on the path between the big garden and the greenhouse. The weather continued to deteriorate and he felt a few scattered raindrops. Oh dear.

He unhooked the solar charger from the clips and stuffed it back into his pack. He looked up to see one of the doors on the nearest building open and a young woman wearing a large hat emerged. Then another, and several more, young and old, following on. They were all wearing hats.

He continued northward, hoping to cross the path of someone he could ask about the gates. It was getting noticeably cooler now that the sun was completely obscured. He passed a hedge just north of the gate and encountered a group of children sitting in a semicircle in front of a young woman. Everyone in hats. How odd this is, he thought.

George was too far away to hear what they were saying, but he could see her gesture from time to time. She didn't appear to notice him, though, and he thought it best not to interrupt them.

On the other side of the grassy area where they were sitting was another building George hadn't seen before. It was almost as tall the main building, which now loomed in the background. George counted what looked like five storeys. He figured he must be nearing the north edge of the property.

There was another gate here on the west side of the complex, with a path that led directly to yet another new building. This one was much smaller than the others and looked more like a shed. A small group of workers emerged from the barn-like structure door, pushing carts and bins containing what looked like gardening tools. George changed directions and approached them, hoping to learn a little more about, well, practically everything.

"Looks like rain," said George with a smile as he approached the first man he met.

"Yes, thank Anna," replied the man.

"Can I answer a quick question for me?" he asked the worker. "I need to leave. Do you know who can open the gate for me?"

"You really want to go through all that trouble?" asked the man.

"Uh, what sort of trouble?" George replied, suddenly worried that he might not be able to get back in.

"You have your re-entry number and your clearance card, of course?"

"Oh, gosh, do I need to have those? I just couldn't find mine. Do you know where can I get another copy?"

"You'll have to speak to someone in Resources. In Building One. Main floor."

"Thank you for the assistance," said George. Leaving the compound without these items suddenly seemed like a very bad idea.

Feeling rather deflated, George trudged back to Building One under a stormy sky. He passed dozens of people—hundreds, even—on his way there. He saw them up in the fourth and fifth-floor windows as they worked, and he watched them step out of the first-floor doorways onto the main plaza and smile at each other in the falling rain. Most of the people he saw gave him a friendly smile or a tip of their hat as they passed. There was something mildly unnerving about all this niceness.

A dark-skinned woman at the main reception desk directed George to the Resources office, which was just around the corner from the desk. The Resources department was bustling with people. Some waited in queues; others filled out forms or handed in résumés. A dozen or so people stood in front of a desk under a sign that said LINE UP HERE.

Behind the desk, a gray-haired woman listened to their stories and directed them to the appropriate "teller." These tellers, as she called them, were separated from their clients by what looked like a Plexiglas barrier. From behind it, they provided advice, directions, or other assistance.

When George reached the front of the line, the gray-haired woman motioned for him to stay where he was while she finished writing a note of some sort. A moment later, she motioned for him to step forward. "Sorry about that," she said. "I needed to finish something up. Now, how can I help you?"

"Hello," he said. "My name is George Gunderson." He leaned a little closer to the barrier. "I'm a time jumper. I've just arrived."

"Well, it is a pleasure to meet you, Mr. Gunderson. Welcome to the Enclave," she said, opening up the binder on her desk. "I have a form here I'd like you to fill out, please. When you've completed it, please take it over to counter number three—right over there—and the teller will be able to help you out. Do you need a pencil to write with?"

"Yes, please," said George. This was all very old-school.

She handed him the pencil and the form, which was filled with questions about whether he needed accommodation, meal coupons, skills training, medical assistance, help with banking, job opportunities, or other social assistance. A few meal coupons sounded good right about now.

An hour or so later, he had completed his orientation interview at counter number three and was sent up to the cafeteria on the mezzanine for his first proper meal in the 25th century.

"May I join you?" asked a voice beside him.

○ ○ ○

My name is Kaedra Wen," she said, extending a pale hand, palm down. She sat down across from him and he noticed how extraordinarily pale and pure her complexion appeared. Even her eyes seemed to sparkle with a rare brilliance.

George was a little taken aback by the gesture, so he cupped her hand in both of his, "Pleased to meet you," he said. "I'm George. George G."

"I am told you know him?" she said.

"Yes," George replied. "He and I used to work together and we became friends."

"That must have been a long time ago."

"It was. He was with me during the Omega Event."

"Ah, the Great Fall. So, you are one of the Ancients! I am honored."

"As am I."

"I like you," she said with a smile.

She looked into his eyes with a placid gaze. She was about 40. Quite beautiful. "What brings you to the new world?"

"Oh, I'm restless, I guess. I always seek out the new."

"Ours is a peaceful place, George G. We welcome you."

"Thank you. Would you like half a sandwich?"

"No, but thank you for asking. Please enjoy it."

"And how do you know—uh, forgive me, I don't know your customs—how do you know Andrew? Do you call him Andrew?"

Kaedra smiled. "You knew him as Andrew, we shall speak of him as Andrew," she said. "He doesn't use that name much, but I have seen it before. In fact, it is written on the birth certificate of my daughter," she said candidly. "Her name is Ceryl Wen."

"Well," marveled George. "I'm pleased to hear that. That's a lovely name. I have so many questions," he said. "I hardly know where to start."

"I usually start with whatever is most important," she offered.

"Fair enough. I'm thinking of going for a long walk outside the Enclave—you know, outside the walls. Have you spent any time out there?"

"Oh yes," she said. "I used to live out there. Where do you think you'll go?"

"Well, I don't really know what's out there."

"Have you been to the old city?"

"You mean Trenton, right?"

She nodded.

"Not yet. Is it a place with visiting?"

"That really depends on what you want to experience. There's a lot of crime in the city, and a lot of hunger and pain. It's dangerous. But if you're up for it, there are things in the old city you just can't find anywhere else. Marvelous things. Music halls and art galleries. Wondrous machines." She smiled ruefully. "As you've probably noticed, we're not big on machines around here. But we are of the new world. The machines and the monsters, they are of the old ways."

"I'm very curious about the new ways," said George. "Can you tell me more about them?"

"As Annatarians, we have guiding principles, passed down from long ago. These are the teachings of Saros, older than the old books and truer than the Ancients knew. He shared these truths even with those who would not listen and, lo, they fell into the darkness and were lost.

"But the truths and the deeds of Saros were not forgotten. The storytellers carry these great truths now and forevermore in their hearts and share them even now, as the end of the great age approaches, as it has been foretold."

"So," asked George, "what do the storytellers say about the world outside the Enclave? How are they different? Why do you separate yourselves from them and their ways?"

"They who live outside these walls do so because they do not know or refuse to follow the path of Saros who knew the ancient ways before the world fell into darkness. It has been shown and is now well known, for example, that extended exposure to the light of the sun is dangerous to life. It burns the skin, it kills the plants, it takes the life from seed and soil. Yet in the cycle of day and night, it is essential, too, to the plant and seed and to all that grows. In all there is, this is true. The One teaches us of The Two. It is the naked reality and the paradox that these two great truths are made as one. And in the sun remains the one true light that guides and sustains us all. Those who relied instead on the artifice of artificial light found only darkness in the night of the Great Fall. And it was the Great Fall that taught us that the darkness that becomes light is Saros' true state, just as the silence that becomes the phonograph becomes Saros' true voice. The mystery of the miracle is that both parts are true and so we learn and we teach by the Ancients' rule.

"We sing of Timeless in the Sun,
The wise and gracious one,
Who leads us through the darkest night,
By his eternal light.
Total Mass in the Sun,
The keeper of the day,
Who illuminates our memories,
By the light of his true way.

"Our storytellers have told us this since the time of the Ancients and we teach it to our children, knowing it to be the truth. So, we dance in the night, and we plant when the life-giving rains fall upon the ground, and we shield our vessels, our bodies, from the killing rays. But those outside the walls, with monstrous blue or reddened skins, they do not heed the words. They slumber still."

"I see," said George.

"The lessons they taught had been told and retold countless times by the storytellers. Their words had outlasted the magnets and machines of the old world.

"The words in the old books faded, false and corrupted by time the taker. The storyteller's words are always new and real and true. They are the givers."

"I really appreciate you taking the time to answer so many questions," said George, as he picked up the last piece of his sandwich. "I just have a couple more. Why don't you guys use electricity? Or computers?"

"Those who lived through the times of darkness taught

us that dependence on that which we cannot control is folly. And when failure strikes, it strikes out at electricity.

"These things, and the impermanence of all forms of technology, have taught us that the truth that never fades is the one borne on those things that survived the Great Fall, born of beliefs that challenge the old."

George listened, fascinated by the oddness of it all, as she went on to describe how, ever since the climate change events of the 21st century led to the worsening effects of solar radiation, the population of most of the developed countries in the world began engineering skin cells to have more melanin as a way to combat the cancers.

The additional pigmentation, she explained, became a checkbox attribute for unaugmented workers seeking a genetically desirable mate, especially if it was dark enough to permit working outside during the day, as those in the laboring class had to do.

Thus, she said, ten generations later, pale-skinned people who didn't have the luxury of a pit to plug into had been all but bred out of the gene pool.

The Augs apparently considered sun-damaged skin a symbol of barbarism and primitivism. Skin as smooth and perfect as possible was the mark of elite class refinement.

They favored selection by way of engineering. It was considered a sign of beauty and an indicator of affluent status to have perfect skin and a pure complexion, as who else could afford to not have to work outside?

The Havenites, too, were careful to avoid the killing rays. Saros set an example by always wearing a wide-brimmed white hat when he ventured into the gardens or onto the court-yard to make a pronouncement. He encouraged his followers to embody the Havenite principles of fairness and purity and follow his example.

Havenite children, she explained, were required to wear their wide-brimmed hats while outside, and most of the Storytellers, teachers, and outdoor workers did, too. There was no sense in burning.

George still couldn't get over the primitivism of it all. "I am curious as to why your community doesn't avail itself of all the modern conveniences and labor-saving devices that are available. Don't you think you would enjoy having programs, machines and robots taking care of menial day-to-day tasks? It's a mystery to me."

"These are not mysteries to us," said Kaedra. "We were shown the signs during the Great Fall. From that silent dark-ness came the light of Anna's teachings."

"I'm still puzzled," said George. "The Augs have these cerebral enhancements that make them a lot smarter. Don't some of your people get envious of the fact that the Augs have intellectual capabilities and opportunities you don't?"

"It is rare, but yes, it does happen," conceded Kaedra. "In fact, my own son made that choice. His father was *furious*. You see, it is our view that *they* are the ones who are dis-advantaged. They are the ones who will suffer most when the lights go out, as they will again, when this age ends as the last one did."

"Where is your son now?"

"I honestly don't know. His father sent him away last year,

along with the woman he was with and their child. I haven't heard from them since then."

"I'm sorry to hear that. And how do you feel about that?"

"I am also sorry. But they made a choice to live outside the community and in conflict with our beliefs. And so, they must live with the choices they've made."

"Before he left, my son told me he sought to know *why* things work as well as *how* things work. Our storytellers could not appease him with their tales or teachings. I don't view that as a failing on our part, as much as the fact that he somehow failed to be able to see the beauty in why things are as they are, and the purpose in how things work as they do. Beauty and purpose.

"You know, some look out and see the same old world. Others see it and understand that the rules have changed. When a system fails, there may be darkness or there may be chaos. The world rights itself, if we let it, all in good time.

"When Saros showed us the true ways of Anna, machines were not needed. Enhancements and augmentations were not needed. The world does not need more complexity. It does not need more of anything except love and understanding. So, we look and we see love and share our stories of that understanding."

All this airy-fairy stuff was getting on George's nerves. He didn't want to offend her.... "But," he countered, "the world has some very real problems. There's pain and hunger and poverty out here, you know what I mean? There's crime and hatred and corruption. What about the greed that comes from a world addicted to growth, or the pain of those who struggle to cope with their losses? How does your belief system help you with that? What are you actually doing about any of it?"

"What we choose *not* to do is as important as what we do. We choose to not be slave-workers for lazy elites. We lead by example. We are teachers, we are learners. We are healers, benefactors, storytellers. We can only set an example of a better way. The world that fell was one polluted by greed and inhumanity. The world needs generosity more than profits now."

When their lunch together was finished, Kaedra bade George farewell and returned to the House of Wen.

With his newly acquired exit pass and re-entry code, George walked across the courtyard on his way toward the south gate.

o o o

19

Visions of the End of the World

As Above, So Below.
—HERMETIC PHILOSOPHICAL MAXIM

On the far side of the courtyard, a crowd of Havenites had gathered—a shifting sea of wide-brimmed white dots beneath the overcast sky.

"What's going on here?" George asked one of the onlookers—a very tall and thin young man. The man was in a group of people all dressed similarly, wearing leaf-green clothes and those wide-brimmed white hats. They looked a little like a patch of flowers growing out of the concrete courtyard.

"It is a rare and special day," he said. "His Eminence, Saros, is speaking. He says 'the natural order of life is one of renewal.' He says we should see ourselves as we are now, not as we once were."

"Seems like good advice."

Saros was quoting from the Annatarian Doctrine now.

"To walk bravely in the shadows is to be prepared when darkness comes, as it surely will, for so it has been foretold."

"Those who fail to learn the lessons of the past will have their chance again, in the new age ahead."

George hadn't walked far when he heard the sound of running feet on the gravel walkway. He turned and saw someone in a white hat running toward him. It was Kaedra.

She rested her hands on her knees for a moment while she caught her breath. "Whew. I'm glad I found you."

"What's wrong?"

"Oh, nothing, really. I spoke to Saros after his speech, and he told me he has decided to go away on one of his vision quests. He said he might be gone for a year or two. So, I thought I might go on a long walk. Are you still on your walkabout?"

"Yes. As soon as I get through those gates, I'm officially in unknown territory."

"Can I join you?"

"I'd be honored. Do you have your exit and entry passes?"

"I do indeed. And a few other things."

An hour later, they reached the outer wall. George entered his passcode and, as the gates opened, he looked back at the buildings in the distance. It still seemed impossible to him that his old friend had a relationship—a child, even—with a woman like Kaedra and a place like this. He had all of this and had just given it up. Unbelievable. Andrew held the keys to a remarkable legacy, yet seemed to care so little for the people that were part of his own past. Just like his father. George wondered if he would ever find what he was looking for.

George was full of questions. "You don't mind some more questions, do you?"

"Of course not. I have some for you, too," she said with a smile.

"So... I'm not exactly sure what the people in your community believe. I get a sense that this religion of yours might have started as an overtly existential humanist philosophy, but it seems to be mixed with an animistic sort of 'all life is sacred' neo-Taoism; this holistic earth-religion appears to be at the root of your spiritual belief system."

"We call ourselves Annatarians," Kaedra replied. We believe in the teachings of Anna the all-knowing, for to be like her is to be wise and pure."

"I also can't help but notice that your society has turned a deep green, in the ecological sense. Technology and industry seem to have more or less fallen out of the average person's life. There are manufactured products around, but not a lot of stores or well-dressed people."

"The world outside, I'm afraid, is not all like that," she said. "Our community is deliberately low-tech. I can tell you, it was a quite a transition for me, when I first met Andrew, or as we now know him, Saros. I gave up on the world of smartphones and laptops and coffee shops, in favor of Saros' vision for a more sustainable world. You might think it's better or worse here in the outside world. I don't know. I can only tell you that we have made the House of Wen a peaceful place—

and that is in itself a remarkable achievement in a world where relentless progress is paid for by the currency of conflict."

"Speaking of currency, I haven't seen a lot of money or even bartering around the Enclave, for that matter. No offence intended, but everyone I met there looked a bit like they were slumming—the overall style was kind of a shabby chic."

Kaedra laughed. "To be truly sustainable," she said, "society must learn to love simpler things—those that are well-worn, used, and recycled. We live according to our belief that the goal of sustainability is be happy with less, not more. The ego always wants more. But history has shown the folly of going down that path. There can be no peace when we want what the other has. It never ends. So, Anna guides us to a different path."

She pointed to a row of houses ahead. "It's the reason we live in a separate community. We understand that not everyone wants the same thing—we just try to set a good example. If these people need to be cerebrally augmented to afford their fancy house, or they decide to get some sort of genetic modification so they can stay out in the sun longer, that's their business. We believe in what they call the plain old human. Our humanity is what defines the best in us."

"No one that I've seen so far has any obvious genetic modifications."

"I think you'll find that things are different in the big city. It's been a while since I've been there, but there are a lot of poor people, lots of big problems. It's very hard to interact with the cerebrally augmented people. Mostly, they are crazy for money. They treat the worker class very badly. I hate to say it, but I've never met an 'Aug' who wasn't an asshole."

"I guess that's par for the course, I dunno."

"Par for the course?"

Oh, that's a reference to a game called golf."

"Hmm, never heard of it."

"I'll bet you there are some Augs out there who play a lot of it."

"I had a friend in school who got augmented. She had always wanted to be smart. Well, she got what she wanted, I guess. She moved to 'Aug Town' and went to work in a fancy building where people just stayed plugged in all the time. We didn't really talk much after that."

"That's a pity."

"Yeah. I think it's fairly common in the bigger towns, I dunno. We should take this road and head south, I think."

o o o

George remembered his school days. He had always wanted to be thought of as smart, too. That's why he had worked so hard to become an expert programmer. People respected a great programmer, just as women responded well to a sharp dresser or a great kisser.

He pointed to a self-driving van as it rolled by. "Hey, there's a car!"

"That's the first one you've seen?"

"Well, you used to see lots of them everywhere, but since I got here, I haven't seen anyone driving."

"The world of the Ancients must have been quite a place."

"It hasn't been that long. I would hardly call a few hundred years ago 'ancient' times."

"They seem ancient because of how much things have changed since then. How much the Augs have changed, in particular. The Ancients and other less-skilled workers are essentially their slaves. It's pathetic, really."

"They probably have robots they treat even worse."

"I'm not so sure," Kaedra said. "I've seen the way they treat their robots, showing off the features of some shiny new model. They're like fashion statements."

George suspected that Kaedra simply didn't understand that these cerebrally augmented 'post-humans' were operating on a completely different level than the plain old humans.

"It's basically a caste system," he suggested, "where the two groups really don't interoperate on a meaningful level. It's like *Neanderthals* and *Homo sapiens*, except the post-humans are a thousand times as cunning. And the plain old humans see them as cruel, which I suppose they are to those they perceive as vastly inferior."

"It's also interesting that the business class in the big city is mostly comprised of cerebrally augmented knowledge work-ers, while the rural areas are populated primarily by a labor class of plain old humans."

"They treat the worker class badly in some parts," she explained. "And it's really dangerous for a worker to go into Aug town."

"Well, you know, when I arrived, I was treated rather poorly from the get-go by an overtly militarized 'security' force."

"Oh, that's different. Every community has to have its

own private security service. The government forces just don't respond to personal issues. They are busy with the bigger issues."

George found himself recalling the prosperous corporatism of the 21st century with a fondness he had never felt before.

"But that's how corruption begins," he insisted. "When an individual or a group is granted authority, there are always some who abuse the power they have been granted. It is human nature."

"And that is why we are blessed to have the wisdom of Anna to guide us."

"I don't think I completely understand your religion's relationship with Anna. What is Anna?"

Kaedra stopped walking and faced him. "Look, you might not understand much about our culture, but I know you know what Anna *was* and, above all else, Anna was real. Not artificial. Tangibly, indisputably real. And just because the power button was switched off does not make Anna any less real. In fact, I'd argue that Anna is more real than any deity that cannot be proven to exist. Anna, to us, is an ideal. A promise of perfect rationalism. A great teacher. A teacher of humans, but not encumbered by human flaws and foibles. Our chosen one."

George had never thought of the machine in those terms. But, in a way, that was all true.

Kaedra confided that she knew more. "I spent enough time with Saros—when he was known to me as Andrew—to hear the stories of his path from the past, and to learn what

Anna was before it became Anna. I understand you knew of it when it was in the form of a machine—the machine that became a cloud. But Anna, I can assure you, is more than that —as it was *always* more. We think of Anna now as eternal—a perfect example of one who exists beyond the limits of human mortality. Hope incarnate."

"Yes, I understand that, I think. But that is a philosophical discussion. What about the practical issues of how to feed the hungry, heal the sick, enforce the laws, and so on? How do you ensure that your people are being treated fairly?"

"Our elders appoint community leaders, organized into a hierarchical form of local self-government, with a council and what is called a 'Supreme Order.' These parties protect our interests and disseminate the knowledge that informs our beliefs and guides our actions. Ultimately, the elders look to the teachings of Saros and the wisdom of Anna for guidance."

"But how do you fund your community? How do you pay for things?"

"We don't pay; we don't trade. The earth is good to us; we plant and grow, we give and receive. Everyone shares. When there is plenty, we share; when there is little, we help those less fortunate and conserve together. Ours is not the selfish way."

George had many more questions about enforcement, punishment, and a hundred other topics, but he got the sense that Kaedra was looping back to familiar positions on comfortable topics. He decided to change the subject.

"I am curious about some of the practical matters of your ways and your choices. I know, for example, that some of your buildings are powered by geothermal energy. And there many other kinds of sustainable energy sources that you could be using: wind, water, solar, and so on. Why, then, don't you use more electronic devices?"

"You might as well ask us, 'why are you not more like those who desire to be more than they are?' Why are you not like those who plug into their devices every chance they get, who cannot or will not live without their augmentations? Why are you not like *them?*"

"We do not speak of it often, but the truth is: our little group has what I can charitably say is an uneasy interaction dynamic with society at large. We built the walls around our haven to minimize the potential for volatile and possibly hostile interactions between our group and the surrounding communities. Before those walls were built, there were conflicts. In areas of high transitional volatility, where two or more groups competed for resources or recognition, the situations worsened. The elders in our group decided to see what would happen if we segregated ourselves. They found that the situation improved. Our people were happier and more comfortable if they didn't have to interact with a group vastly more economically differentiated or intellectually advanced than they were. Not only that, but the 'intellectuals' didn't seem to be happier or healthier, anyway. They suffered more from stress-related sicknesses, unhappy marriages, political dissatisfaction, crime, and other problems. So, we kept to ourselves and we like it that way. The ethical decisions based on those differences have both protected and isolated us—kind of a mandated primitivism. Of course, we do not force people to be here. If they want to go live in the pits and pursue that lifestyle, that's their choice.

"Now, my personal view is that the goal of my own life is not simply to seek comfort and happiness. That is much too simple a goal for me; I also realize that others might not share *my* goals. I believe strongly, as does Saros, in a community based on the principle of the natural way. From comfort and happiness, greater aspirations may spring. Good things can grow from such fertile ground."

○ ○ ○

On each walkabout that she took, Kaedra always tried to see the world with new eyes—as it was, not as how it had been. On this walkabout to the Outlands, Kaedra saw things through the eyes and experiences of her companion, too. George was just so different from the other men she knew— so different, even, from his friend Andrew. She wasn't sure whether she liked his rough style, but he did have a unique perspective and wasn't shy about sharing it with others.

Following the signs leading to the downtown area of Trenton was easy, but Kaedra wanted to take a more a more scenic route. As the downtown area was less than twelve miles from the Enclave, they were already within the city limits by the early afternoon.

For so much of her life, Kaedra had focused on trying to see the true nature of all things. Now, here was someone who so readily saw the false nature of so many things. It was both surprising and refreshing. And comforting, in a way, to know that the world of the elites seemed just as vacuous and specious to him as it did to her.

When they walked past some of the grand old buildings in the university district, he asked her what she knew about Thomas Edison.

"We know of one whose name is Timeless in the Sun."

"Our story-song teaches 'Time is all that's in the sun.'"

"Thomas Alva Edison, that's him."

"Yes, we sing of him as 'the wizard of the park' who gave us sound and light and projections in the dark."

"Well, the park you sing of is just about twenty miles northeast of here. We could easily walk there and back in a single day."

"I'd like that."

The old city of Trenton wasn't what George had expected to see. At every turn, as far as the eye could see, every storefront was boarded up. Every retail outlet was abandoned and piles of garbage were everywhere. On several of the downtown streets, messy camps of tents and lean-to shelters occupied the sidewalks and homeless people huddled around burning refuse bins. But on many of the streets it was eerily quiet, like a ghost town. No cars, no smiles.

The stately old buildings in the historical districts were still there, albeit with few less statues than there used to be. Heroes come and go, he supposed. Even in the once-bustling financial district, all the ground-floor windows were boarded up or papered over, with long-fade offers for lease or sale.

The street people seemed to avoid the richer district, and George soon saw why, as Kaedra pointed to the drones buzzing overhead. The area near the old bus station George had known as a youth had been completely redeveloped and now appeared to be a multi-storey housing tenement block. Like many of the other buildings in the area, it was mostly derelict now, covered in graffiti, with all buts the highest floors' windows boarded up or covered with cardboard and paint.

They saw no moving vehicles, but passed an occasional burned-out shell of a car or, more commonly, an abandoned delivery truck.

"Let's go this way," suggested Kaedra, pointing toward the river.

The area near the Delaware river was better. The once-scenic waterfront area certainly different than George remembered, but it looked relatively inviting, compared to most of the areas he has seen so far.

"Shall we go that way?" he asked.

Kaedra shook her head. "It's not safe. Too many addicts down there."

Across the river, the buildings on the Morrisville side had gotten a little taller and, sadly, almost all the trees along the waterfront were now gone, but by and large, it was still a mostly unremarkable, occasionally picturesque riverside area where there were still vestiges of the old grandeur George had known in the past.

"That's Morristown, there, isn't it?" asked George, pointing to the buildings.

"Oh, it's not called that anymore," replied Kaedra. "That's the old colonial name, isn't it?"

"I dunno," said George. "It was named after Lewis Morris,

I seem to recall. A governor, or something like that, I think. What's it called now?"

"A bunch of the areas along the river were redesignated with indigenous names," explained Kaedra. "I'm not too good at remembering them, unfortunately. We just call it the west bank—or, on this side, the east bank."

Even on the Trenton side, the riverfront road was one of the most pleasant areas George had seen so far. The grandeur of the old buildings had not completely faded away in the harsh light of the homelessness and inequality of the mean streets they had passed through on the east side. There were even a few well-dressed people on the streets here and there.

George had expected to see ridiculous levels of excess and affluence, or perhaps horrific levels of poverty and decay. Instead, on the way back, he and Kaedra shared some of their food with a hungry young woman outside the art museum. The young woman, who introduced herself as Miley, was upset that, even with her new cerebral augmentation, she still couldn't find a job.

She did, however, share her thoughts about the museum's exhibit of images from Leonardo da Vinci's "Visions of the End of the World," a series of works that she told them had been recently been recovered and restored to the digital archives. It was, she said, a series of inspired drawings of the apocalyptic culmination of the concept Leonardo called *Saper Vedere*—Latin for 'knowing how to see'— in which he depicted the laws of order, harmony, and proportion that presided at the world's creation as manifestations of the immaterial forces in the cosmos, invisible in themselves, but revealed in the material things they set in motion.

Both George and Kaedra were fascinated not only by the young woman's enthusiasm for the subject, but also because it gave them a better insight into the way the 'augmented' mind worked. Her insights seemed, at least to them, remarkably profound.

She explained how she had plugged in to her augmentation unit before studying the drawings and paintings in the Leonardo Da Vinci archives. What struck her most, she said, was the apparent fascination Leonardo had for "mirror writing" in the final years of his life. She wondered if this propensity was simply a clever method the left-handed genius had devised to avoid smudging drawings and smearing inks, or whether there was some deeper meaning. Perhaps he had crossed over into a mirror world and was communicating from there. Perhaps he intuitively suspected the existence of parallel worlds. Or perhaps he saw in the mirror the two faces of the soul; the duality of all things. It didn't seem a coincidence that Leonardo had just completed work on the design masterpiece now known as the "DNA staircase" in Château de Chambord, where he worked on his Visions of the End of the World.

"So," George asked, as tactfully as he could, "is your augmented intelligence always online?"

"Oh no," said Miley. "In fact, it's offline right now." She explained that going offline—or unplugging, as she called it— had initially caused her to become quite agitated. The lack of all that extra input caused her to feel anxious and unwell.

"However," she said, "I have since learned to use it as a way of mentally shifting gears into a more relaxed and meditative state. Now, if I could just find a job, I'd be able to truly relax."

The way she spoke reminded Kaedra of her own daughter. "Well, it was a pleasure to meet you and we wish you success in finding the job you seek." Kaedra held out her hand.

Miley's hand was shaking as she reached out. "Thanks again for the meal. Goodbye."

When she had left, they sat quietly for a moment. Finally, George broke the silence. "I think I've seen enough of this area," he said quietly. "I would like to do some more research before setting out again, to know more about where to go and what to expect."

"I understand," said Kaedra. "I know a different way we can go back. Shall we try that?"

"Sure."

By mid-afternoon they were once again at the gates. George and Kaedra used their entry passes to return to the Enclave.

○ ○ ○

20

Brainbooks and Transhumanism

> *If we can just get better men, we can make better developments.*
>
> —HARVEY FIRESTONE

The display on the console flickered to life and a well-dressed man with dark skin appeared on the screen. "Welcome. Would like to understand more about services available here?"

"Yes."

"Let's start by learning a little more about you," said the on-screen avatar. "You can speak the answers or press any selections that apply. Let's begin."

'Tell us about yourself' appeared on the screen, with a series of prompts. "Please explain why you're here and we'll figure out how to help you," said the avatar.

A series of suggested topics floated by on the screen. When did you arrive? Why are you here? What do you need?

"I, uh, arrived recently," said George, hesitantly, "as part of the Andna jump program. I'm not sure whether I'll be staying here or not. I may want to jump forward again at some point. I guess I need a place to stay."

"Thanks for the information," said the avatar. "We just have a few more questions for you. What kind of job or career experience do you have?"

"I'm a development engineer, systems architect and programmer."

"Last question: have you undergone any type of cerebral or physical augmentation?"

"Wait—what? What do those terms mean?"

"Cerebral augmentation is a mandatory requirement for many career choices these days. This quick and painless process greatly enhances your mental capacities and opens the door an expanded set of workplace options.

"There are many varieties of physical augmentation but generally, these modifications increase strength, speed, visual or auditory acuity, stamina, or other physical attributes. Many veterans have undergone one or more of these augmentations and may qualify for additional benefits or special reclassification."

"Tell me more about cerebral augmentation requirements and options."

A lavishly produced video began to play. "Your future awaits," said an attractive woman. "Dare to have it all." Ask for more information on full virtualization, said the screen.

"Tell me about full virtualization."

Now came the hard sales pitch. "High costs of living got

you down? Frustrated by limited housing options or health problems? The ultimate solution is now available. It all goes away when you Go Virtual."

"Tell me more."

"It's easier and more affordable than ever to Go Virtual. And just think of all the money you'll save! Sign up today."

"Okay, how do I sign up?"

"It's easy to sign up. Simply sign the required forms and, as soon as your finances are approved, your new life can begin. Note that full virtualization is non-reversible and non-refundable. You must be at least 21 years old to participate."

"How much does it cost?"

"Going virtual is now more affordable than ever. The basic cost is now just $180,000."

"No way," said George, "I can't afford that."

"Great news! Pre-approved bank financing is available OAC. There's also a timeshare program available for those who want to reduce their monthly payments. Would you like to know more about Virtual Timesharing?"

"Yes."

"With virtual timesharing, you decide how to spend your own free time. Any free time you don't spend helps pay off your loan. It's the easy and affordable way to go virtual. Don't delay. Your future awaits!"

George tapped on a link labeled *Terms and Conditions*, which led to a 48-page license agreement. He spent a moment scrolling through the dense legalese before deciding that it might be wiser to spend a little time learning more about the "Go Virtual" technology and "Virtual Timesharing" program specifics before delving into the license agreement. Besides, he hadn't eaten all day. He dug into his pack and pulled out his recorder, two energy bars and a bottle of water. He unscrewed the cap and took a long drink, then began reading. His planned trip back to the old city could wait. This was much more interesting.

The app detailed the various technologies involved. The Extensible Holographic Augmentation Device (EHAD), it explained, is the primary front-end interface. It allows the duplication or transference and enhancement of synaptic functions via, as the name implies, extended by the device. This technology, which can only inaccurately be termed a "machine," is more properly categorized as a neural transmitter with chemically actuated bio-link software and hardware. It is commonly referred to as "wetware."

During the initial phase of the Virtualization process, the entire state of the brain is digitized and uploaded from the host to the EHAD. Once uploaded and initialized, the EHAD can extend its awareness to incorporate other nodes. The app invited the user to refer to the following topics for more information about these terms: Content, Resolution, Quantization, Bandwidth, Rights, and Simultaneity.

The key compromise made during this synaptic transfer process, it seemed to George, was made apparent by numerous references to "quality levels" and "quantization technologies." The virtualization system worked by creating internal models that were essentially resolution-independent and then subsampling them down to deliver a multisensory user experience that ran smoothly, given the processing limitations of the virtualization host's processing capabilities—which were nothing short of astonishing to George. That quantized sky in the demo video might only have 10-bit resolution, but it looked amazing.

The demo video explained how VirtuaCorp scientists developed the system. They began by asking: If one were to accurately reproduce the functionality of the brain, what level of sensory output would be sufficient? They set a baseline equivalent to 60 frames-per-second, 32-bit color ultra-hi-res vision, full-fidelity 24-bit audio and touch, taste, and smell experiences that were, they claimed, designed to be indistinguishable from those of a healthy 20-year-old human.

Simply put, these were very high-resolution renderings indeed. However, although the VirtuaCorp technology produced a very accurate simulation in environments with low to moderate computational demands, it tended to bog down when presented with a more computationally challenging environment. The video showed dramatic frame-rate degradation during an otherwise-impressive virtual sandstorm. Due to the design requirement to have a consistently smooth user experience, dynamic degradation of the user environment became a necessary compromise—at least with the early prototypes. You'd still experience the sandstorm, but your virtual eyesight would see it with something no better than 20-20 vision—still good, but not quite a sharp as the system was otherwise capable of delivering.

Subsequent versions of the system were developed that achieved "superhuman" levels of quality. While there was considerable market demand for such capabilities, the easy-to-spot differences between full "ultra-resolution" output and mere 20-20 vision during computation intensive segments were deemed far too obvious for it to ever become ever become a mainstream product. The researchers eventually came up with several quality enhancement algorithms, which reduced hardware demands, with varying levels of quantization artifacting.

The most highly quantized level of digitality compliant with the standard favored high frame-rates over high resolution. Scenes would typically exhibit minor visual and auditory anomalies. A stormy Venusian sky, for example, might take on a rather checkered look, as continuous tones were deemed a waste of valuable bandwidth. Similarly, high-fidelity audio was reduced to a level where some aliasing was permitted, but considered within acceptable limits. But given that George hadn't experienced a Venusian sky, stormy or otherwise, this didn't sound like a deal breaker.

Another alternative was to undergo augmentation, which essentially put a smart-chip in your brain that increasing your cognitive abilities. This was, as the presentation mentioned several times, a requirement these days for many career categories, for all but the most intellectually gifted individuals.

There were a few popular models of synaptic enhancers on the market, and both proprietary commercial and open-source encoders.

The most popular design was REST, so named for its ability to record and encode synaptic topology. It improved upon earlier designs by combining low computational overhead and exceptional programmability. Using a form of fractal compression, the REST user's synaptic maps were encoded as resolution-independent routines that could be recorded and recalled at will.

A less expensive system known as synaptic topology augmentation routines (STAR) also became popular due to its low computational overhead and exceptional programmability. It, too, used a form of fractal compression to record synaptic maps as resolution-independent routines—albeit with a higher amount of aliasing than the REST system.

There are a relatively small number of fundamental connection types in the brain, through which all information is channeled. Of course, there are many millions of each of these types of connection.

The cyberforming process of mapping the synaptic connectors into neural wetware—sometimes referred to a 'n-coding' —exploited the discovery that information can be quantized down to levels understandable and retainable by an individual not linked to the Net. This naturally revolutionized the educational system and virtualized the mentor system.

These technologies built upon a previous breakthrough, when it was discovered that the synaptic functions could be digitized and uploaded to a host system.

The consumer-level program, the system explained, employs optimized routines for the most common routes; that is, mapping the synaptic pathways in heaviest use. The others are quantized down from 10^{32} to a poly-molecular level of 10^{24} bits.

There continues to be a community of "retro" n-coding enthusiasts who claim to enjoy the older low-res encodings.

Large libraries of low-res recordings of mostly technical braindumps are available in online repositories such as ncoders.co.uk and neuronauts.org

Crowdsourced funding is sometimes used to pay for the n-coding of high-resolution versions of some of the more popular low-res archives, with some authors releasing materials in both the new and retro formats.

Commercial repositories on n-coded braindumps have mostly moved to a subscription model, after a market flirtation with one-off sales of NFT-protected 'brainbooks' in the early part of the century.

Saros despised all such technological augmentations and he counselled his followers into taking a hard-line stand against them. Users with any form of augmentation, whether it was of the pangenetic type or otherwise, were shunned and demonized.

The Havenite community was dedicated to the imperfect 'purity' of the plain old human (POH). Time jumpers from the past were welcomed and arch-conservative ideologies were supported by both the rules and the culture.

o o o

You have requested information about HAVEN. Please choose from one of the following topics:

- Heuristically Adaptive Virtual Environment
- Heuristic Audio/Visual Exonet
- Holographically Augmented Visual Experience
- Host-adaptive Virtual Network

The Heuristically Adaptive Virtual Environment is a head-mounted neuro-synaptic recorder/player that non-invasively augments the intelligence of the wearer.

The ability to interpret and record brainwaves led to the emergence of a new class of head-mounted devices that were essentially 'smart helmets.' With one of these devices, one's synaptic functions, including thoughts, feelings, dreams and other sense memories, could be digitized and uploaded to a host system, or to another individual.

Research and Development

Around the beginning of the 24nd century, there had been a great deal of research undertaken that sought to determine what level of description is sufficient to accurately reproduce the functionality of the brain. Experiments were performed in which every motor neuron, myofiber, and Schwann cell was accurately modeled—in other words, a very high-resolution recording. Although this produced a very accurate simulation, it was deemed far too computation intensive to ever be a marketable product. The International Standards Organization (ISO) eventually published a set of specifications for several levels of quantization, standardized capabilities and safety measures, and ways of dealing with various issues such as synaptic overload.

Over the next century, progress continued to be made on such devices until, by the early 25rd century, smart helmets were replaced by much less intrusive tech that not only played back previously recorded synaptic events, but dynamically uprezzed them as well.

It has since become popular for hobbyists to work and play with the neural code recorded with the older, technically obsolete models, many of which contained endearing quirks or unusual user interfaces. Many thousands of examples of this early n-code are publicly available, both in native libraries and in translated and upscaled formats suitable for playback on more modern n-coding devices.

As well, most n-code device manufacturers provide application programming interfaces that support interoperability between the most popular standards.

The most highly quantized level of digitality allowed under the ISO guidelines produces only minor visual and auditory anomalies that are barely noticeable in most cases. Rapidly moving water, for example, might exhibit visual artefacts such as a slightly checkered look when experienced at the lowest quality level. Similarly, audio could be recorded with sufficient fidelity to model the vibration of individual air molecules, but to what end? It merely has to be good enough to meet the limits of human hearing, really.

Other senses were modeled this way, too, with the predictable improvements in the quality of this or that as the never-ending parade of updates and upgrades went on.

During quantization, the 'realism' of the neural recording is reduced to a level where some aliasing is permitted, but considered within acceptable limits. Newer models support the ISO's highest quality level, which is considered 'virtually lossless.' There are also a few technophile models that exceed the highest established standard of quality—at a premium price, of course.

Older n-code stations have been gradually called in and re-established. Without data compression, the complexity of the data in pathway would lead to unacceptable bandwidth problems. Therefore, the one in most common upper-echelon use today utilizes an improved n-code that allows massive neuro-parallelism.

Host Module

Most commercially available HAVEN modules are playback only. The actual recording is done via a larger and rather more complex device known as the Host Module (sometimes derisively referred to as "the Pit"). During the neuro-synaptic recording process, a variety of sensors are employed to detect and capture neuro-chemical state changes, brainwave patterns, temperature, and other data.

The host module HELIOS (Heuristic Environment Link / Integrated Operating System) works within the Hosted Adaptive Virtual Environment to augment the subjective experience of reality.

21

Neogens and Havenites

 Schrödinger and Heisenberg and their followers
*created a universe based on super imposed insep-
arable waves of probability amplitudes. This new
view would be entirely consistent with the Vedantic
concept of All in One.*

— WALTER J. MOORE

George had always known that there was a danger of becoming dependent on the availability of electricity in an increasingly technology-driven society, but it seems hard to believe that it could come to *this*. These virtualized people were one hundred percent dependent on their electronic host. It would take a lot to convince him that such a risk was worth taking.

He spent a great deal of time researching the various augmentation options and the risks versus rewards of pangenetic versus wetware enhancement technologies.

The aspect of the wetware approach that really sold him

was the direct access to a private AI programming interface. You had to plug in an 'e-net' external cybernetic interface whenever you wanted to use the higher functions, but it was far more future-friendly than the purely genetic enhancements, which were basically just 20-point IQ boosters. To take full advantage of the e-netic interface required one to learn the unit's idiosyncratic programming language, but for those who did, it was extremely powerful and versatile. The other feature that really struck him as a killer app was the ability to record anything and everything. Recording his own dreams was the feature George had always wanted. The fact that virtualization also included cerebral capacity augmentation was just icing on the cake. He signed the digital form approving his willingness to undergo the irreversible procedure.

Due to the 'buyer's remorse' laws, the system explained to him that the procedure took seven days before it became irreversible. The first six days were essentially orientation sessions, designed to introduce what would, on the seventh day, become his new reality.

Day one was heavily on the practical side, emphasizing ongoing benefits such as cost savings in housing and food, which would be limited only by the sophistication of the available code libraries—and, for a programmer like George, he could add his own libraries if the existing database of virtual homes, meals, vehicles, sexual partners, and other optional selections proved inadequate. It seemed unlikely this would be an issue.

As the orientation session progressed, George was amazed by the variety of domiciles available: luxury homes, castles, yachts, mushroom huts, cloud cities and more. There were even domed cities on space stations or other planets. No problems there, thought George. Food, too, was entirely optional. You could virtually eat—and taste, the program promised—a wide selection of meals designed by world-class chefs, enjoyed in the virtual environment of your choice. It was your choice of meals, beverages and desserts, in your favorite surroundings. The system promoted its rich depiction of reality, but sold itself by making things like hangovers optional.

Day two emphasized the social aspects of the program. You could interact with "plain old humans" as a hologram, or you could engage with other virtualized entities as, well, pretty much whatever you wanted to be. A demo showed how you could virtually modify your looks, your voice, your strength, height, weight, skin or hair color, or anything else. There were a lot of incredibly attractive people in the system—and more than a few freaky avatars that were distinctly non-human. Amusingly, the orientation session presented a number of statistics showing the percentages of virtualized men, women, and "others"—and then compared these numbers to the original genders. Perhaps unsurprisingly, the numbers didn't match. They weren't even close.

Day three continued selling benefits of the program with the exploration of intra-personal dynamics in business. Here, the training program seemed uniquely customized to map to George's own career interests. He wondered how a person who was, say, an architect or a banker might experience the tutorials. The program mentioned these disciplines, but only in the context of how a knowledge worker such as a software engineer might interact with them on a business level.

It was fascinating. If anything, the potential for an individual to make and maintain a vibrant career appeared to be enhanced by the ability to effectively network with others and rapidly interact with them on a global basis, without the usual limitations imposed by need for sleep, or the practical limitations of working with teams halfway around the world, in places like India or Australia.

Day four drilled further into the potential to grow a business as a virtual entity. It was here that George began to see the scope of exactly how the virtualization company's business model worked. As a Virtual Capitalist, George could build an expertise portfolio by paying for the necessary skills and connections he needed to acquire. Similarly, his specific skill set as a systems architect or a programmer became a monetizable skill-set 'snap-in' that others could license—or they could choose to work with him directly as a contractor-for-hire. By licensing a large number of 'snap-in' customers, one could achieve a scale of business that an individual worker could never hope to attain.

Day five began with a recap of the 'snap-in' concept and then explained how to manage business and personal affairs on a truly massive scale that 'plain old humans' couldn't hope to match. A key concept in the world of Virtual Capitalism was that of the business avatar. Essentially, it was the old concept of business AI applied to a virtual likeness of one's self. This instance of "you as a service" handled the mundane chores, freeing up bandwidth for activities worthy of the executive self's attention.

On day six, the orientation shifted direction a little to

discuss the more esoteric extra-cost options. Accessing the AI application programming interface was, for George, one of the most compelling possibilities and here the extent of what was possible was laid out in considerable detail. You could purchase altered states of expanded consciousness. Many of these were marketed with lurid imagery and provocative names, such as Ayahuasca VX. There was even one going by the name of Virtual Godhead.

The orientation session only mentioned them briefly but in fact, organized religions were onboard with the program in a major way. All the major organized religions had a presence. You could download the Catholic VX virtual experience and experience communion inside a truly grandiose cathedral or be an onlooker at key liturgical events. Some groups went much further. A common feature of many western religions was the presentation of showy "virtual Bible stories," allowing you to personally witness various events from the Bible. Christian churches tended to focus on New Testament stories, while the Jewish experience was big on fire and brimstone, with spectacular production values in epic scenes such as the story of the Noah's ark, or Moses parting the Red Sea. The Church of Latter-day Saints declined to participate, but a splinter group appropriated the officially deprecated term 'Mormon' and released the controversial Mormon VX, complete with a tithing feature that automatically transferred funds from your bank account to the group. Islamic interests were represented by a deep-dive depiction of the Five Pillars of Islam. And for those into eastern traditions, there were plenty of options, too: a strongly cosmological take on Hinduism, a virtual monastery experience in Buddhist VX, and so on. One of the most surprising was the Taoism VX, which was presented in a way that managed to be both respectful to the subject matter and surprisingly modern in its approach to the three ideals of Taoism: acceptance of your life, finding peace, and enabling possibility.

Indeed, although George wasn't even remotely religious, this message, more than any of the others, made a lot of sense in the context of the Virtual Experience.

And when at last, the lessons of day six were over, the presentation sought confirmation for the final step: to give up one's body on the seventh day and step into the light.

Before George pulled the proverbial trigger, he made sure he'd read all the fine print in the license agreement documents. However, despite George's prodigious ability to consume mass quantities of technical documentation, he wasn't as big on legalese. He found himself scrolling rather half-heartedly through the 48 screens of the virtual timesharing conditions and terms of use.

It's a pity that George didn't read the entire document more carefully, as he ended up agreeing to a decidedly dicey scheme in which George's virtual self became a gig worker during his spare time, to a maximum of 32 hours a week.

On the surface, it seemed like a pretty sweet deal. As soon he signed up, the $180,000 fee was treated like a loan, which was immediately paid to VirtuaCorp and George was moved to the front of the line for full-service virtualization. His $180K debt would be paid down by $1000 per 8-hour day, up to that 32-hour per week maximum. Piece of cake!

As George quite regularly pulled all-nighters and 80-hour work weeks, this 32-hour-a-week condition hadn't bothered him at all as he skimmed through the terms—especially when he read that his virtual gig-working self could pay off the debt *while he slept.* It was, he would soon learn, what virtual gig worker George had to do to pay those bills that proved a tad problematic.

You see, the way the virtual timesharing program works, a third party can occupy your virtual self during your downtime. This means that your avatar is under someone else's control. Your actual awareness of what is going on is limited to whatever you can remember of the dreams you experienced at that time. Some people don't remember their dreams at all, so this isn't a problem for them. George, however, was something of a lucid dreamer, and he remembered a lot of what went on.

There were rules about no illegal or immoral activity, but they weren't strictly enforced. Many of those who hired virtual freelancers were primarily interested in having sales

people who could convincingly pretend to be excited about—
or at least interested in—a deal designed especially for suckers.

It was a lot like acting in commercials, pretending that
the mail-order shoes were comfortable, or this-or-that was an
investment opportunity too good to pass up.

The day after he signed on to the virtual timesharing program, George woke up after a night of dreaming about selling "come-as-you-are" teledildonic pleasure packs for lonely
women.

○ ○ ○

Did you know?
You can literally make money while you sleep! Sign up for
virtual timesharing today.

○ ○ ○

22

The Far Reaches

—CARL JUNG

One of the most difficult aspects of virtualization to get used to was the fact that the virtualized persona may or may not have a matching corporeal body. Most of the time, when dealing with others, this wasn't a problem. Most interactions in the business world were either with duty bots or virtualized entities. And most of those were spammers or scammers anyway.

Duty bots were much better than even an augmented human at housekeeping tasks and the scammers typically took advantage of this familiarity by posing as a duty bot, needing access to your financial service handler, of course.

On the rare occasions when one of these bad actors—typically masquerading as a new and supposedly essential service of some sort—wasn't automatically detected when it tried to request permissions to your household or business account, those with access to cloud-based virtualized entities had a distinct advantage in dealing with them. The scammers would reach out and your agent's management interface would run its request in simulation mode to figure out what it was trying to do before taking the appropriate action. The vast majority of the time, that stopped the attack cold.

However, human hosts without such automated help systems were at significant risk, as the most successful scammers avoided interacting with duty bots entirely and relied exclusively on social engineering attacks. Humans were so much easier to fool.

There was no point in interacting with systems that can automatically detect and defend against a bot-based scam when you can rely on the same old social engineering tricks that have, for hundreds of years, been duping users into granting access to their private accounts and valuable resources. As it had always been, it was just a numbers game.

Being fully augmented prior to virtualization had become popular with the over 40/under-60 crowd, whose minds were still coherent and cognizant enough to take full advantage of the augmentation, although their bodies were not what they used to be. For some of these folks, the body was worth keeping, but the costs to do so were so exorbitant that many decided to go strictly virtual.

The government incentives were attractive. The fully virtualized personae contributed to economic growth and environmental recovery, cost practically nothing in terms of health care and welfare, and didn't require the brick-and-mortar infrastructure or roads and highways that those in meatspace did.

Nevertheless, the vast majority of people who went virtual did so, at least initially, with the "team-up" option. This option—often provided as part of a money-back-guaranteed 30-day trial—allowed the corporeal body to continue living with the virtualized persona, as cohabitors of the self. And, to be fair, not everyone prefers the virtual life. But George did— at least most of the time.

He figured that he could send his body forward time and time again, which had so far resulting in a better virtual ex- perience in every case, while maintaining a virtual presence in each time period with the infrastructure required to support the requirements of cerebral augmentation.

The other advantage was that his virtual 'agents' would continue to work in the cloud even if he was, for whatever reason, unable to connect to his e-netic interface module. It seemed like the best all-round option.

There were, of course, ad campaigns galore touting the ability to go fully bodiless. These appealed mostly to those with chronic or terminal illnesses. There were "leave your body behind" ad campaigns targeting the very old or the supposedly ugly, as well.

George was neither of these things, but he always liked to preserve his options.

One of the ways George did that was by setting up bot- based agents to monitor topics, people and places he was interested in. He had bots monitoring jobs and development projects at NASA, ASTRA, Andna, and several contractors for the government that he had done work for over the years. His bots also monitored people and aliases he wanted to keep track of: all of the old Andna employees who were still alive or virtualized were on the list, as were old friends, their kids, old girlfriends, and on and on.

Originally, these intelligent agents were touted as a way to expand one's sphere of influence, allowing one to conduct business from beyond the corporeal domain. However, negotiations conducted exclusively by agents tended to devolve into stalemates, as multiple bots pitted their algorithmic wits against each other, pitching increasingly dubious compromises to one another. Worse, all the 'state of the art' bots had computational defenses that kicked in whenever they determined that a deal was being brokered by a bot instead of a human host. It wasn't long before bots simply wouldn't deal with other bots. Worse, human hosts had to prove they weren't bots just to initiate a negotiation. It was a war of the haggle-bots.

The absolute worst thing about augmentation was the silence when the system went down. It didn't happen very often, but every few months, the cloud-based agents would blink off for a few seconds. The psychic silence during that period was terrifying. These service interruptions usually occurred when the system was offline or became unavailable during upgrades. Whatever the cause, it was like a black hole that sucked all the interestingness out of the world for a stark and terrible moment that seemed much longer than it really was.

Having an e-netic module on at the time buffered the impact of this emptiness, but it was still a shock when it happened.

23

The Fallen Temple

2999

Jumping forward five hours or 500 years felt exactly the same. First, there was a ring of light, then a sudden blink. And of course, when an object or person appeared, there was a sudden breeze as the air was displaced. And so, when Saros, in a swirl of dust, was suddenly swept 564 years forward by the machine, he didn't realize at first how far forward in time he had traveled.

But here he was, suddenly unsteady upon a broken platform with his once-proud golden robes flailing in the wind, surrounded by the remains of his fallen temple and a destroyed accelerator.

It took him a moment to reorient himself to the new environment. Suddenly, he was facing a crowd of people taking photographs. And, as they lowered their cameras to gape in awe at this sudden manifestation, he realized that they were all hybridized humanoids with gills and fins. Monstrous fish people—and tourists, to boot. He stared in disbelief at a t-shirt one of them was wearing. It was a picture of the temple—*his* temple—as it used to be. The destroyed temple was now a tourist attraction!

It seemed like nothing short of karmic destiny that a crowd of the very people that Saros feared most now surrounded him, taking photos of him as if he were an ancient artifact.

As a crowd of curious tourists gathered, he stumbled in his shock and surprise. A kindly couple reached out to steady him. One held onto his arm with his finny fingers, while the other took hold of his gloved right hand. Horrified by their monstrous appearances, Saros pulled his hand out of the glove and gestured menacingly with his wizened right hand.

Just then, a pair of security guards pushed through the crowd. "We'll take it from here," the tallest one said as the other directed the crowd toward the old Annex for the next exhibit. The guards pulled Saros into a small office in what had once been a storage room.

"Okay, buddy," said the tall one. "Why are you assaulting the guests?"

"And what's with the getup?" the other added, eyeing his golden robe.

"This place is my home and these are my clothes," declared Andrew indignantly. "I own this property."

"Yeah, right," scoffed the shorter guard.

"Who's in charge here?"

They took Saros to meet the exhibit director, whose office was at one end of a patio just west of the main building. The office was in an irregularly shaped concrete building that had the telltale textures of a 3D-printed structure. The guards marched Andrew past kiosks selling hats, t-shirts, souvenir guides and—for some reason—Chinese food to a waiting area near a glass door. One stayed with him while the other entered the office. A moment later, the door reopened and the director appeared. He studied Saros' face and clothing for a moment and then motioned the guards to bring him into the office. They sat him down in a chair across from the director's desk and turned to face the director.

"We'll be outside if needed," the tall guard announced and they left the room.

"Good afternoon," he said, extending a hand. "My name is Torres. I'm a director here." He studied Saros' eyes for a few seconds and then spoke again. "So, they tell me you are carrying no ID. Can you tell me your name?"

"My name is Andrew Stern. Andrew Oliver Stern."

"I see," said the director. "And what year were you born?"

"2005. April 21."

"That's a very long time ago," said the director, looking up from his screen with a look of mild annoyance on his face. "And how old does that make you now?"

"Well, that's a difficult question to answer," Saros said hesitantly.

"Yes, I'm sure it is."

"Look, there must be legal documents showing the owner-ship of this property, yes?"

"I'm sure you can get a copy of the land title down at City Hall. But you still haven't explained where you've been or what you've been doing for the past 990 years or so. I'm sure you can understand my skepticism upon hearing a story like yours without any proof."

"Yes, I appreciate that. However, if there are legal records, I'm confident they will prove my story's authenticity."

"Without conclusive identification, sir, that may be difficult. Are you sure you have no ID?"

Saros shook his head.

"Would you have any medical records or, I don't know, a bank account or a license of some sort, to back up your claims? Or tax records. You must have tax records."

"I don't think so." Saros had a sudden idea. "Say, do you have any pictures or records or history books about this property?"

"Mm, yes, I have a few books here. We sell them, you know." Torres retrieved a pair of books from the shelf behind him and set them on the desk. He hunted for a moment and then pulled another one off the shelf and pushed it toward Saros. "These are a few of our most popular titles."

"Great. Let's have a look." He paged through the first chapter of the book entitled *The Haunted Enclave.*

"Aha, this is promising. Ridiculous title, though."

"Oh, I wouldn't say that. The old enclave has been the site of many spooky sightings over the last thousand years or so. It's what the place is most famous for."

"There's actually a scientific explanation for all that," said Saros, paging through the second book. "It was declared a secret—a top secret, in fact—a long time ago, so I don't know exactly how much I'm allowed to tell you about it. Does the United States government still exist?"

You mean the ROA? It's the Republic of America. It hasn't been called the U.S. for many, many years. But, yes, there's an American government. It always was a constitutional federal republic, wasn't it?

"Yes. So why the name-change from USA?"

"When D.C. became a state, there was a lot of noise about the status of Puerto Rico. Hawaii was threatening to secede, as was California. So, when the 'stripe' states above Texas there decided they didn't want to be 'united' any more, things were so messy, it was just a way out of that mess, I suppose. 51 stars would've looked terrible on the flag anyway."

"There," said Saros, pointing to a photo of Isaac Stern shaking hands with a government official. "That's my father. He's the one who willed the estate to me. The estate was— and should still be—in my name."

The director had clearly had enough. "All right, well, you leave the guests alone and go get your land title, then get back to me, all right?" he said, somewhat patronizingly. "County records and property tax records should be easy to obtain down at City Hall. You can just get in touch with them and get the information you'll need to validate your claim. You might want to find yourself a good lawyer, too. Those photos won't stand as proof in court."

Torres closed the books and put them back on the shelf.

"It's a bit ironic," observed Saros, "that you have all these books about this place, when there were no books allowed here at all."

The director looked mildly intrigued. "By the way, if what

you say *is* true, we'll probably end up being business partners. The old temple is quite a tourist attraction."

"I'm very pleased to hear that. Anyway, thank you for your help," said Saros. "Do you know where the nearest financial institution is?"

"There are terminals in all the buildings here." He opened the door and pointed to a seating area visible just beyond an open archway on the other side of the patio. "There's one right there by the food stand." He pointed to the Chinese Food sign.

"I think I need to sit down with someone in person," said Saros.

"Good luck with that," said Torres. "You'll probably have to go into the old city for in-person banking."

"I'll do that," said Saros. "Thanks."

As Saros exited the office and stepped back onto the breezeway, he heard an old-fashioned radio station playing over the PA system. "You're listening to Radio WONE 101.1 FM: The One." He wasn't sure whether it was real or a vintage recording, but it was as ridiculous as that book title, he thought. And books!

○ ○ ○

As Saros began looking into what happened to the Enclave property, AndnaCorp's business assets, the House of Wen, and the other vestiges of his former life, he discovered that the properties and assets had been transferred to his heirs as the estate went through probate, following his disappearance and presumed death. Fortunately, Saros found that several of his former bank accounts and investment accounts still existed and contained money—in many cases, greatly aided by the compounding interest that had accrued over the years.

He was able to gain access to the funds with the help of a lawyer.

Saros was just as disinterested as ever in the ever-changing challenges of technology, so he decided to hire a technical expert to assist him in getting his life back in some semblance of order. The temp agency recommended a woman named Shan as a temp worker to assist him with finding an executive assistant/technical expert, who could help him put his life back together.

"This is definitely a job category where you need to pay the premium to have an intellectually augmented aid," the temp said.

"Absolutely not," insisted Saros. Unfortunately, he soon discovered that non-augmented tech experts simply didn't exist. It was one of those categories where you simply had to have the equivalent of a Master's degree in computer science, and all Masters-level programs had augmentation or a 235+ IQ baseline as a prerequisite.

When this baseline was added to the hiring profile, the name "Frank Folupa" rose to the top of the list.

And when the time for the remote hiring interview came up for Frank Folupa, the person who showed for the video interview was none other than his old friend George.

Saros, who was present but offscreen during the interview process, recognized George immediately, but didn't let the temp know that Frank Folupa was obviously a pseudonym.

And despite Saros' occasional disagreements with George in the past, he couldn't deny that his old friend had the technical chops he was looking for—and then some. In fact, George was one of the key people he had hoped his new tech expert would be able to find. And here he was.

○ ○ ○

Saros was delighted to find George, of course, but he couldn't help but be curious as to how and why a tech expert as accomplished as George would be available. He advised Shan that this was the candidate he wanted and instructed her to offer Mr. Folupa five per cent more than the median rate for positions of this sort if he could start immediately following the interview. He agreed. And with that, Shan's work was done. Saros thanked her for exemplary service, tipped her well, and sent her on her way.

Appearing on the video feed, Saros didn't let on at first that he knew who he was. "Hello Frank," he said. "I'm your new employer."

George didn't skip a beat. "Hello, old friend. I didn't expect to see you today. Is this just an amazing coincidence or have you been looking for me?"

"Both, really. Would you like me to call you Frank, or do you prefer something else?"

"Please bill me as Frank Folupa and refer to me that way on my eval. Other than that, let's be ourselves."

"Sure," said Saros. "There's a lot to catch up on. So much has happened."

Never one to resist stating the obvious, George asked Saros

point-blank why he was no longer at the Enclave. "It's gone, George," he said sadly. "It's nothing but a goddamned tourist attraction—and apparently has been for a long time. So, I guess it was all for nothing."

"That was back in—what? The twenty-third century?"

George explained to Saros what he'd been up to since they'd last met in the Enclave. He knew that Saros was not a fan of human augmentation tech, so he didn't belabor that point. Instead, he focused on his time-jumping exploits, which he knew Saros shared an interest in and enjoyed.

George described his *modus operandi* since then. His chief innovation was his practice of leaving Qmunications devices at the jump points he'd passed through, along with virtual copies of himself as agents at the same jump points. "That way," he explained, "I can communicate with my agents at all the jobs they are working on, and the agents can forward my funds and find new contracts when they're done. And they can earn virtual timesharing credits for me, too."

He also explained what he called Squirrels and Dodges.

"Squirreling, as I call it, is an investment strategy I've had success with, where one invests in long-term plays, then races ahead to capitalize on the investment without the wait. They don't all play out of course, but the risk assessment algorithms help to minimize the risks.

"Short squirreling is a tactic of short time jumps of 1 or 2 years at a time. The idea is to stay long enough in one time period to safeguard your caches. You also take the temperature of what has been happening to adjust your predictions. Then you time jump again.

"Dodges are jumps in which the primary goal is to avoid the heat of scrutiny, by, say, evading a statute of limitations. By keeping a low profile long enough, a dodger can maximize the value of a shady investment while minimizing the risk of legal ramifications."

This reminded Saros of a question he'd been meaning to ask George. "Hey," he said, "are there any other jump stations still in operation?"

"Well," said George, "It has been several hundred years. I would imagine the technology has propagated since the old days. There are probably jump stations all over the place. Or more likely," he added, "on people's *wrists* all over the place."

"I know of three for sure," he said, "and I suspect there are a few secret ones in use by the military, too. The best equipped facility I've seen is the one in Houston, at the ASTRA lab. It's beautiful—or at least it was when I last saw it. God knows if Houston is even above water anymore. Anyway, back in the day, it was pretty spectacular. You should see that place."

"There's also the one under the old Andna building, you know, under your temple."

"Not any more, I'm afraid," said Saros. "I don't know what happened, but that one is in ruins. It's literally a tourist attraction. I was thinking of ones that are believed to be currently active."

"Well, there was at least one in China, which I haven't seen personally. I knew a few of the people who worked there, though. I can look into that."

"What about the one in Novelty Hill?" asked Saros.

George shook his head. "Nope. I don't think you're ever

going to see that one up and running again. It was badly damaged in that bomb blast."

"Do you have any way to access the jump-station at the ASTRA facility in Houston?"

"Well, I don't, but George Gomez does."

"Who's George Gomez?"

"That's Frank Folupa's *other* alias."

"So, you could help me make a jump?"

"I could. I might even make one myself, if you can get us to Houston."

"I can do that."

"I could use a holiday."

o o o

After a 14-hour electric plane flight, George and Saros finally arrived in Houston. "Wow, that should have been like a three-and-a-half-hour flight," grumbled George.

"What do you think? Do you want to take a taxi to the ASTRA facility?" Saros asked him.

"You're probably not going to like hearing this, man, but there really aren't any taxis any more. It's all done via autonomous shuttle these days. But no worries. I've got a token set up to book it and geolocate me. It'll be here soon. Uh, 14 minutes, it says."

Almost exactly 14 minutes later, an autonomous shuttle pulled around the corner, flashed its lights twice, and smoothly braked in front of them. The passenger-side door lifted like a falcon wing. They threw their bags in the back and climbed aboard.

"It's a 22-minute trip on the fastest route, it says," reported George. "Do you want to go straight there, or have a bite to eat first? I'm starving."

"Let's eat first. I don't eat animals anymore, but other than that, I'm quite flexible."

"Man, I eat nothing *but* animals." George said with a grin. "Don't worry, I know just the place."

"Hey shuttle, take us to the nearest Chicago Dogs."

George plugged in his e-net and spent most of the trip browsing for information about recent changes at the Space-Time Center. "Hey, apparently, they just finished a big sea-wall to protect Houston. It says that Galveston is almost completely underwater these days."

"Too bad. I used to like Galveston."

"Hm. Says New Orleans is underwater, too."

"Betcha Miami is, too."

"Uh, yep. And they *did* have a big seawall."

The shuttle pulled over and opened its falcon-wing door.

As they stood in line to order at the Chicago Dogs restaurant in the food mall, George pointed to the animated menu. "See that Tofu Veggie Dog? That used to be Li Yan's favorite here. You'd probably like that. It's really good."

"Sounds perfect. You know, everyone used to fast once a week at the temple, so I kind of got used to doing that. It's really hard when you're not used to it, but it gets easier."

"I know what you mean," said George. "Around my parents' place, we used to *feast* only once a week. That was rough, too. Hey, you don't mind if I have a beer, do you?"

"Gosh, no," said Saros. Same old George.

"Do you want one? For old times' sake?"

"Sure. For old times' sake."

○ ○ ○

Later that night, and several beers later, Saros—feeling more like Andrew than he had in a very long time—watched with amusement as George, now festooned in an off-white cowboy hat he'd somehow acquired during a trip to the washroom—rode a mechanical bull as a trio of women applauded. Typical.

○ ○ ○

The next day, Saros and George traveled via autoshuttle to the ASTRA lab at the Space-Time Center. Both of their IDs were preapproved for transit, just as George had arranged. "Do you want to go first or second?" George asked.

"I've always been lucky," said Saros. "I should have kept an exact count, but I must have done more than a hundred jumps and I've never had a problem—I'll go."

George looked it up. The records from Saros/Andrew totaled 136 jumps in all.

"I'll stay behind, just in case something goes wrong," said George. "Good luck. See you on the other side."

Two minutes later, a message arrived on George's com link. It was from his agent. While searching the dataverse for recent activity by persons of interest, a new record had popped up. It was from an unknown party who had been sending messages to several of George's associates. It had been flagged as noteworthy because there was a hundred percent overlap with people that Saros knew. This person was trying to find Andrew.

Seconds later, another message appeared. George had been CC'd, but the agent's message was intended for Andrew.

"Andrew," it said, "I think someone is trying to find you."

375 years after Andrew learned of Marjorie's death, an orbital shuttle docked with the space station she had been working on. The space station hatch opened and an astronaut emerged, gliding weightlessly through the open hatch. The astronaut's helmet glass reflected the interior lights of the airlock area as she made her way inside, pulling herself along the zero-G railing to the airlock control panel. She pressed the interlock control button to seal the exterior door and waited until the red light turned to green. Another astronaut peered through the window of the interior door and smiled. When the air pressure in the cramped chamber reached one hundred percent, the shuttle astronaut opened the inner door and the astronaut from the station removed her helmet. It was Marjorie.

"Ready to go home?" he said.

"You bet," she replied.

24

Trapped

DO NOT FOLLOW' the message title said when it arrived along with a skull emoji.

It was accompanied by a message that said it was from Andrew@ASTRA. "You are receiving this automated message because you have been designated as an emergency contact for Andrew Stern. Something has gone wrong and Andrew is unable to communicate. Emergency Protocol is in effect."

Following this text was a diagnostic data dump with the coordinates, time, and jump-gate ID. He had been attempting to jump from the Houston jump-station, and had been headed for Dec 31 of the year 2999.

Emergency Protocol was auto-invoked if the "OK-clear" status flag was not set after a jump by a transit pod, or if a Bubblecraft failed its post-jump diagnostics.

George reviewed the error log on his com link, then swapped the data onto a larger screen for a closer look. The troubleshooting agent explained that there were many reasons why this error condition could occur—and almost all of them were very bad news indeed.

An obstruction, such as a wall or pile of rubble that intersected with the path of the incoming pod was often cited as the most likely cause, but high radiation levels, poisonous air, flooding or excessive hot or cold conditions were all designed to invoke Emergency Protocol.

It was, the agent said, also possible—albeit highly unlikely—that the error condition could be the result of a component failure of the field generator itself, although the prejump initialization routines were designed to catch errors of this type before a jump.

The agent explained that the temporal portal was now flagged as no longer operational. Any attempt to initiate a jump from that location would now invoke a dump of the error condition, with diagnostic data and a log containing the target date, location, and environmental data. Fortunately, the fact that the log's data fields were not empty was an indication that the pod was in one piece. And, most likely, that meant that Andrew was still alive. The error log listed the target time as 12:00:00 on 2999-12-31.

"Please use an alternative jump-point if you are headed this way," suggested the agent. "And always share your target date with others so they can find you. Jump safely."

As George thought about what to do, another message arrived on his com link. It had the same ID as the earlier message from the 'unknown party' sender. This one, however, was coded as a holograph. George tapped *Accept*, not knowing exactly what to expect.

"Is that you, George?" asked the holographic entity.

"Who is this?" inquired George.

"It's me, Marjorie."

"Marjorie who?"

"Marjorie Blint!"

"Wha—?! B-but we were told you were dead!"

"I know, sorry about that. It was a top-secret mission. We were testing the Starjumper out there on the other side of the moon—just to keep it out of sight, you know?—and I had to jump forward. They couldn't very well explain what was going on if an astronaut goes up and doesn't come back, so a fake cover story was created that blamed a depressurization incident. The craft—supposedly with my body in it—was said to have burned up in the atmosphere, just in case anybody went looking for evidence."

George could hardly believe his ears. "Oh my god," he said slowly.

"I wasn't allowed to tell anyone. Not even my husband. I did, however, have a hundred-year limit on the non-disclosure of the truth. We had an arrangement to meet all set up."

George frowned. "This is a lot to process."

"So, my time's up and I'm trying to find out what happened to Andrew. I tried sending him a message using an anonymizer, but I never heard from him. I CC'd you on that one, by the way."

"Yeah, I saw that, but unfortunately, I couldn't tell who it was from. The message was truncated."

"That's a shame. I've had agents out there looking for him for quite a while. He's like a ghost. There are references here and there to his activities from the period of time following my mission, but they were all dead ends."

George explained the whole Saros situation and why he wasn't using the name Andrew anymore.

"Well, maybe he will start using it again when he hears from me. I don't fancy being known as Mrs. Saros."

"So, how did you find *me*?"

"Oh, you weren't that hard to track down. The records on Karl and Li Yan pretty much led me to you. But Andrew's records seem to have been deliberately falsified."

"Heh, yeah, that was my work. Funny—I thought I had protected myself at least as well as I had obfuscated him."

"Well, the fake employment records and the surname 'Gomez' were unexpected, I admit."

"That's me—just an old farm worker from way back."

"What's interesting is that there was nothing at all visible in your records until recently. Did something change a couple of weeks ago?"

"Yeah, I signed up for a thing called virtual timesharing."

"Well, your data appeared in the population database right after you did that, I guess."

"Typical."

"So, you know where he is, then?"

"Uh, more or less. He just did a jump that we're trying to track."

"But he's okay, isn't he?"

Yeah, I think so. You *just* missed him. I'm sure he'll be extremely happy—and at least as surprised as I was—to hear from you. Where are you, anyway?"

"I'm in Houston. Just got here."

"Wow, so are we. Strangely enough, he's been at the family property—you know, the old Andna site—in Princeton almost the whole time. He's been there more or less continuously since you two lived there, as far as I know."

"So, is there a way I can contact him?"

"Yeah, we've got the transit module communication link working. Do you want me to send him a note to let him know that you're alive?"

"Um, no, let me do it myself. I want to see his reaction."

"Well, I'm sure hearing from you will absolutely blow his mind."

"I can hardly wait."

"I'm at the ASTRA lab, downstairs on level one. Do you want to meet me down there?"

"Yes, I'll be there in about 20 minutes."

○ ○ ○

When Marjorie arrived, George explained the situation to her. Despite his best efforts, she was clearly alarmed when she read the message containing the distress signal.

"Why hasn't he sent anything else since then?" she asked. George didn't want to admit it, but that *was* worrying.

We'll have to wait until we hear from him to determine when and where you can find him."

A follow-up message never arrived.

○ ○ ○

As George pondered how—or *if*—to try to help his old friend, Marjorie explained more about what had happened to her.

She said had attempted to contact Andrew several times, and was living under an assumed name not far from the Houston Space-Time Center.

George, meanwhile, was preoccupied with questions about what had happened and what to do about it.

Marjorie's sharp intellect impressed George. Very methodically, she went through every possibility she could think of.

"I'm operating on the assumption that the transit pod's manual Qmunications mode isn't working correctly, but the transit pod's automated QM transmitter is okay. The fact that we received a message from it suggests that the pod's integrity has not been seriously compromised; hence, Andrew is probably also okay," she theorized. "That would explain why the automated status report was sent successfully, but subsequent communications were not."

Sounded reasonable.

Marjorie was working through the options in her head. "Hm. If Andrew realized the pod was not working correctly, and switched pods to continue on from there, that would explain why we're not receiving his communications. At least one of us would have to jump there to pick up the new QM module."

"I don't think he would do that," George decided. "Remember, our plan was to be in Houston at noon on December 31, 2999 and stick around for the turn of the century."

Marjorie held up her hand. "Hm. Yes, I think you're right.

Let me think this through again. We can't jump to a period before the breakdown and then proceed to alter the arrival conditions by repairing the jumpgate," Marjorie reminded him. "Otherwise, we will change the timeline directly, which we are strictly forbidden to do. Even indirect changes are believed to be damaging."

George had been cowboying things with unauthorized jumps and skipped briefings for so long, he hadn't heard the bit about indirect changes before.

"We would be allowed to jump to any time *after* Andrew's jump, though, right? We could repair the platform and then everything would be okay again, wouldn't it?"

"Hold on there, chief," George said. "You say 'we' as if you think I'd be coming with you. I want to make it crystal clear: despite our old plan for a New Year's Eve party, I have no intention of jumping into a known dead end, as much as I'd like to see Andrew's expression when he sees you."

This admission surprised Marjorie. "But you build and repair these things for a living!"

"Not gonna happen. I don't like dead ends and I don't like unknown variables."

"Well, speaking hypothetically, then: you wouldn't know for sure whether you will be successful at repairing it—and if you're not, you'd *both* be stuck there."

This got George thinking. "What if one jumped forward *before* the breakdown and did nothing but evaluate the situation until after the main causal timeline had occurred normally?"

"That's a good question," conceded Marjorie. "Anytime

the outcome is altered, it supposedly fractures the timeline, so... I dunno. There have been many debates on this topic. It's hard to predict the consequences of a seemingly small change.

"I was part of a panel of experts reviewing the data from the so-called timeslip tests in 1947," she revealed. "There were some experimental tests in the spring and summer of that year where they were trying to get reverse time travel working using the Everett-Schraeder equations. They never did get it working properly, and there were some casualties, so the government pulled the plug on the tests."

"Eww, casualties?"

"Yes. There was also a huge backlash from the consulting scientists involved with the project. The theoretical physicists thought that it was too dangerous to risk altering history. The engineering team was told to kill the project. They were given strict instructions that it was completely forbidden to even try to replicate the one inconclusive result that was achieved during those initial tests."

"Inconclusive?"

"Yeah, they did manage to make half of the jump platform vanish at one point, and a couple of technicians disappeared, but what happened to them was never discovered."

"Or never disclosed, maybe?"

"Hard to say, some of the military data was redacted and remains classified as top secret, so we couldn't really replicate those findings from the initial tests if we wanted to, anyway."

Marjorie sighed.

"I'll bet you if we tracked down Schraeder, he'd have the information we'd need—if he's still alive, of course."

"Perhaps. I think he's still alive. But he was in the government's bad books for helping me make an unauthorized jump."

"Yeah, Karl was fired over that, wasn't he?"

"And so was I," said George.

"Yeah, that's when it all seemed to go wrong."

"Not entirely wrong. You and Andrew met around that time, didn't you?"

"Yes, of course, not that part. I meant the rest of it. The Cornerstone problems and Andrew's father dying. Oh, that reminds me: you heard about that Fidor guy who supposedly died, right?"

"Supposedly?"

"Yeah. That's what they told us, but you know, I've heard that he was like me, doing secret tests. So, I wouldn't be at all surprised if he's still alive, living under an assumed name somewhere. After all, that's exactly what happened to me, and they told you I died."

"They told everyone that. We all grieved."

"I know, I'm sorry about that. But I did leave an anonymized message for Andrew. He saw that, didn't he?"

"No! I think he thought it was just another condolence. He had stopped reading them by a certain point—you know, he was never very big on electronic communications. He just didn't want to hear the sympathy messages anymore." George thought for a moment. "So, were you serious about trying to track down Karl Schraeder?"

"Absolutely."

"I'll have my agents look into it."

○ ○ ○

Even with his e-net-enhanced IQ, George kept cycling through what seemed to be a too-short list of unpleasant options.

1. Jump to a point before the problem and risk potentially catastrophic consequences;
2. Jump to a point after the breakdown and risk getting stuck there himself; or
3. Hope that there are other technicians there to help Andrew fix whatever problems he had encountered.
4. Send diagnostic tools and equipment that might allow Andrew to fix the problem himself.

Option four seemed most promising. If they could get the Qmunications working, at least they could find out what Andrew's status was.

George asked the ASTRA techs if they had any spare Qmunications modules they could send forward.

"Sorry," said the manager of the tech department. They were all out and the spare parts were no longer available. And he couldn't order them anyway. And, no, he wasn't allowed to cannibalize a working transit pod to pull out its QM module.

"What about a Bubblecraft?" he asked. If I had one of those, thought George, I could send *it* forward, and then Andrew could rescue himself.

It wouldn't exactly be a rescue vehicle, but it would get

Andrew out of this dead end. That is, if it wasn't too late already.

He asked the director of the ASTRA team if such a thing could be arranged. "Sorry," she said. The answer was no.

As it was, with the ability to communicate on the backchannel broken, option three was a complete unknown. That left option four looking like the safest and best proactive choice in a lousy set of choices; however, without two-way Qmunications, it was also highly unlikely to succeed, given that Andrew didn't know much about the technical details. An Aug might be able to figure it out, but not...

Hmm—wait. Maybe Andna's in-house augmentation services were still available. Andrew would just have to get to the Aug lab and run the orientation program. The system bots would take it from there. It was worth a try.

Andrew, he wrote, *hopefully you can read this. We have not received your replies. Backchannel comms not working? Have possible solution. Will send information on how to fix module. If you have trouble with the instructions, go to Aug Lab on L1 Room AL1 and run 'orientation program'.*

Even as he hit *Send,* George knew Andrew was unlikely to choose augmentation. The way George figured it, Andrew was smart enough that he would probably be able to figure things out even if he didn't go through with the augmentation process. But he was also smart enough to realize that it might help.

Marjorie had a different idea. "I'm thinking I should just jump there in person, using the same time factor he used. If I can help him, I should. And if I get there and my

Qmunication module works properly, as it probably will, that will help all of us. And if Andrew is hurt, well, I'll take a first aid kit."

"Worst-case scenario is that I die. That's not a concern after you've volunteered to take a ride strapped to four and a half million pounds of explosives. Best case: I save my husband's life. Best anniversary gift ever."

"So, this is not a hard decision for me—and I don't see any reason to delay, especially if he might be hurt."

The ASTRA staff agreed and the transit pod was moved into position on the deck. George helped her load up the pod with a first-aid kit and a box of diagnostic tools. "Good luck Marjorie—sorry about the New Year's Eve plans," he said as she stepped into the pod. "Don't forget to write," he added as she buckled herself in. She gave him the thumbs-up sign as he closed the hatch and gave it a pat for luck.

o o o

As she sat there waiting for the 10-second countdown to complete, Marjorie wondered if maybe he wouldn't *want* her to jump back into his life—and straight into a dead end—after all this time. Would this—could this—bother him? Bah, she decided. Tough luck if it does. He knew damn well the kind of woman she was. For better or worse. Time to go.

Blink.

Anyway, knowing how he felt would certainly help her decide what to say and how to proceed.

She checked the status. All good. Time for a quick message to George: *Are you receiving?*

Yes! came the reply.

No sign of Andrew yet. Please wait for further info.

∘ ∘ ∘

25

Turn of the Century

It had been almost 30 minutes since the jump and Andrew was still missing. Marjorie sent another status update.

His pod looks OK and has been moved off the jump deck, so he must be here somewhere. Place is dark and mostly empty. Looks like this facility may have been decommissioned. Will report back when I find him.

Reading this message from 564 years in the future made George realize the folly of the endeavor. The risk of the jump-gate being decommissioned was something he should have foreseen. Using a Bubblecraft for any long jump would be—would have been—a much better idea. He had better find Andrew. He needed to ask him if the old Bubblecraft was still around.

Light switches are on a power panel in the electrical room, about ten paces down the corridor, on the left side. Should be labeled, he wrote.

Marjorie was inside the electrical room when she heard footsteps in the dark hallway.

"Who's there?" called a man's voice. "George, is that you?"

Marjorie flipped the switches on the electrical panel and the fluorescent lights in the room and in the hall buzzed and flickered on. Marjorie stepped out into the hall and there was Andrew. They were both a little older than they had been when they'd last seen each other, but Andrew had *never* looked so surprised.

"I—I thought you were dead," he stammered. Tears came to his eyes. "You're alive."

"Surprise."

"I had to go to the... You know that we're... stuck here, don't you? The jump gate's not working."

"I don't want to jump away from here. I jumped here to find *you*. I was just on my way out to the front of the building...."

"I can't believe it," Andrew said. "It's really you."

"It's really me. I should tell George I found you. He's still back there, waiting for a report."

"He didn't get my messages?"

"No. There must be something wrong with your pod's transmitter. Just a sec." She quickly dictated a status message and sent it via the new pod's transmitter.

Andrew has been found. We're both fine. I have much to explain. Don't jump until I have completed and sent diagnostics.

George had no intention of following them. He had resolved to think things through fully before acting from now on. His reply arrived seconds later.

Questions for Andrew: Is the Bubblecraft still working? Is there some way I can get to it?

"These are questions for you," Marjorie said, as she showed him her commlink display.

"Not so close," he said. "My eyes aren't what they used to be. Getting old sucks."

"No, it doesn't," she said, gently squeezing his hand.

"Do you want to dictate the answers to him or should I?" she asked him.

"Would you? I'm no damn good at that stuff."

The answer to both questions is yes. The Bubblecraft was working the last time I used it. It's in my grandfather's storage locker, and I can give you the address and the code to unlock the door.

"You have a Bubblecraft in storage?" asked Marjorie, incredulously.

Andrew nodded. "Surprise."

Sorry for the change in plans, but I don't see any point in me making this jump right now, George wrote.

Three's a crowd anyway. Let me know if you need any supplies, and I'll arrange to have them forwarded to you. I will catch up with you later, once I've retrieved the Bubblecraft. Happy new century!

o o o

Later...

A truck pulled up at the charging station at Menlo Park. The driver's side door opened and out jumped George, making clouds with his breath in the crisp morning air. He plugged in the fast charger and opened the rear doors of the cargo box. Inside was the Bubblecraft. He plugged it into one of the wall-jacks inside the truck and checked the straps, then closed and locked the rear doors. He pulled his hat down and eyed the distant clouds on the southern horizon. This time tomorrow, he'd be in Houston.

Epilogue

Year 3000

That first day after the turn of the century was like the first day of their honeymoon all over again. Andrew was finally reunited with Marjorie and everything seemed right again. This was especially true nine months later when Marjorie gave birth—not exactly in the old-fashioned way, but close enough—to a baby girl they called Lilly.

It took a while, but Marjorie eventually found out about Kaedra and Andrew's names on the birth certificates of Ceryl and Nolan Stern. She gave Andrew a hard time for not voluntarily disclosing this information, but she had, after all, been legally declared dead.

One day, out of the blue, they received a message that had been sent hundreds of years ago. It was from Kaedra. She had continued her journey of personal growth and exploration and had come to realize that acceptance of all people, all beliefs, and all phenotypes was an essential part of that journey. She said she had been inspired by George and a young woman they'd met in a park one day, who had encouraged her to be bold and take big chances. She was doing that now, she said, by taking a leadership role on the Council and permitting Miran to return with honor to the Enclave.

"I hope you understand. I am not asking for permission, for I know this is the right thing to do. Some things are important and this is one of those things."

"Who is Miran?" Marjorie asked.

Andrew explained that she was the significant other of his son Nolan and mother of his granddaughter, Frigg. This also required further explanation.

Andrew realized his reputation as a truth-teller was under serious duress in Marjorie's eyes. But he eventually told her the whole story—about everything.

And so it was that, at the dawn of the new millennium, Andrew, Marjorie and little Lilly watched the sun come up together.

o o o

THE END
of Book Two

BOOK ONE - HELIX

Mathematician Susan A. Everett, intrigued by Einstein's statement that time "is like space"—that is, not just a single dimension—guides a team of researchers to a breakthrough reinterpretation of his famous space-time theory. With the help of code developed by XAVR, an AI-based programming genius, this unlocks the secret of time-travel, but in the forward direction only. What they don't know is how their experiments affect the future world. The story focuses on the life-changing experiences of the first people to go forward, when there's no going back.

BOOK THREE - HELIOS

Welcome to Seahaven, where an unprecedented solar storm is about to create havoc. Elsewhere, a top-secret quantum radar program provides a 'carrier wave' signal, enabling the creation of a temporal displacement field synced with a specific location on or off the earth—but a coding error has far-reaching consequences. With this tech and the knowledge of where and when a disaster known as the Omega Event will occur, the chrononauts attempt to change the future. Or is it inevitable?

www.ingramcontent.com/pod-product-compliance
Lightning Source LLC
Chambersburg PA
CBHW071431200726
48294CB00002B/595